A
Perfect
Ten

D0995249

Other books by Chris Higgins

A Perfect Ten

Chris Higgins

Hodder Children's Books

A division of Hachette Children's Books

Copyright © 2008 Chris Higgins

First published in Great Britain in 2008
by Hachette Children's Books

The right of Chris Higgins to be identified as the Author
of the Work has been asserted by her in accordance with the
Copyright, Designs and Patents Act 1988

1

All rights reserved. Apart from any use permitted under UK
copyright law, this publication may only be reproduced, stored
or transmitted, in any form, or by any means with prior
permission in writing from the publishers or in the case of
reprographic production in accordance with the terms
of licences issued by the Copyright Licensing Agency and may
not be otherwise circulated in any form of binding or cover
other than that in which it is published and without a similar
condition being imposed on the subsequent purchaser.

All characters in this publication are fictitious and any
resemblance to real persons, living or dead, is purely coincidental.

A Catalogue record for this book is available
from the British Library

ISBN 978 0 340 95069 2

Typeset in Bembo by Avon DataSet Ltd,
Bidford on Avon, Warwickshire

Printed and bound in Great Britain by Clays Ltd, St Ives plc

The paper and board used in this paperback by Hodder Children's
Books are natural recyclable products made from wood grown in
sustainable forests. The manufacturing processes conform to the
environmental regulations of the country of origin.

Hodder Children's Books
a division of Hachette Children's Books
338 Euston Road, London NW1 3BH
An Hachette Livre UK company

For my lovely family

Thanks to Jan and Tony,
and to Kate for the title.

The night before the Intermediate, Mike gives us his usual spiel.

'Perfection. That's what we're looking for in gymnastics. It doesn't matter how simple or how difficult your moves are, they've got to be faultless.'

'Yeah, yeah,' mutters Sophie in my ear. Her boredom threshold is super-low. 'We've heard it all before.'

'In your case, Sophie,' says Mike, who doesn't miss a trick, 'that means concentrating on what you're doing instead of eyeing up Jason.'

'Cheek!' she splutters, then adds hopefully, 'Are the boys on tomorrow?' We burst out laughing.

'That's not important,' he says, frowning at her. 'What *is*, is getting a good night's sleep and turning up on time. And that applies to all of you!' His expression changes and he grins. 'We're going to wipe the floor with them tomorrow, you watch!'

We cheer and break up into small groups, heading for the changing rooms, Romilly, Sophie, Hannah and me, chatting together as usual. We're the Jimmies. (Gym-ies, get it?)

I love this bit, the night before a competition when all the weeks of practice are over and your routines are so ingrained in your head you could do them in your sleep. And I do. Them in my sleep, I mean. Maybe that's why I never make a mistake, not like Romilly at last year's Intermediate when she froze in the middle of her floor routine because she couldn't remember what to do next and cost us the team gold. Trust Rommy.

I watch her rummaging through her bag for something, amongst the screwed-up, out-of-date forms she should have given her mother to sign and the piles of unwashed kit. Unlike mine, her mother never goes through her stuff. 'Yes!' She locates the chocolate bar and brandishes it triumphantly. 'Want some?'

'Please.' I slip my top on and sit down on the bench to pull my trackie pants over my trainers. They catch on the soles and I tug them and there's the sound of tearing. Flip.

'You'll get in trouble with your mum,' Rommy says. She snaps the chocolate in two and automatically hands me the bigger half. I'd never do that. I wish I could but I'm one of those people who just has to have the biggest

2

piece, if you know what I mean. Rommy's more generous than me. Plus she always seems to have an unlimited supply of chocolate. 'Here you are, eat it up before she sees you.'

We munch companionably as we gather our stuff together and leave the sports hall, shouting goodbye to Mike and the others. He waves a hand and calls, 'Don't be late tomorrow!' As if!

Outside the leisure centre, Mum's waiting in the car park. I cram the last of the chocolate in my mouth and thrust my arm round Romilly's shoulders, squeezing her tight.

'See you tomorrow,' I say indistinctly through a mouthful of chocolate.

She hugs me back. 'Sleep well!'

I wish. Mum says I've always been the same. I was terrible as a baby, kept them up all night, not like Amber who was an angel and who slept round the clock from day one.

'That's why we didn't have another one,' she'd said over breakfast one morning when I was nine. 'I never had a wink of sleep with you.' Dad muttered under his breath, something like, 'Thank goodness for that, four's more than enough!' and ruffled my hair and called me his 'little contraceptive'. I remember Ben hooting and Amber making sick noises and Mum spluttering, 'Don't say that in front of her!' and I asked, 'What's a contraceptive?' But then everyone fell about screeching like a herd of hyenas, even Zac who probably didn't get it either, so I got cross and took myself off and looked it up myself in the big dictionary. It said 'coitus interruptus', which sounded important but didn't mean a thing to me, and then it said, 'a preventative of pregnancy' and I still didn't see how *I* could prevent a pregnancy, a condition I knew all about because my friend Hannah's cat had just had kittens. But I wasn't going to ask them again because I HATE being laughed at. Thirteen-year-old Amber enlightened me anyway.

'They meant you were such an awful baby they didn't want any more kids after they had you,' she explained.

I was so angry I punched her and she thumped me back, and we continued squabbling in the car on the way to school. I still didn't really understand but now I know Amber had got it wrong. After they had me they didn't want any more kids for one good reason only. Why would they? Their perfect family was complete: two boys and two girls.

And in case you're wondering why I can recall this conversation from four years ago so accurately, it was because it took place at breakfast time THAT MORNING and I can remember ever single detail of THAT MORNING as if it were yesterday. I'd had a

4

disturbed night, and Mum had been up and down to me. I know what it was. I had this comfort blanket sort of thing I used to take to bed with me, and it had disappeared and I couldn't sleep without it. I was convinced Amber had taken it and hidden it somewhere. Anyway, Mum was shattered – it took her back to how permanently tired she was when I was a baby and never slept.

I think that silly contraceptive incident was the last time I can remember Mum laughing out loud.

I still don't sleep well, but that's another story, and at least I don't keep every one else awake all night any more.

Mum leans over and opens the door for me. 'Is she going to let you down again?' she asks, nodding towards Rommy who's cramming her ponytail under her crash helmet, astride the back of her stepdad's motorbike. 'Dangerous things,' she shudders, then says automatically, 'Put your seat belt on.' She ought to make a tape; she says this every time I get in the car, even though it's the first thing I do.

'No! She's learnt it really well this time,' I say, springing to Rommy's defence before I have time to remember my mouth is full, but it's too late. Mum darts a look at me as she eases out of the car park.

'What are you eating?'

'Nothing.'

'Chocolate! It's chocolate, I can smell it! Eva, what have I told you? Supper's ready when we get home and that will spoil your appetite and you'll . . .'

'. . . get spots. I know. Sorry, Mum, it was only a tiny piece.' I lie convincingly. It takes years of practice. You have to with a mother like mine, who sees danger in everything, including a harmless bar of chocolate.

'It's for your own good,' says Mum, peering anxiously from right to left before she edges her way cautiously out into the stream of traffic. 'You want to fit into your leotard tomorrow.'

'I'm not fat!' I object fiercely. Mum sighs and pats my knee.

'No, sweetheart, you're not. You're just right. But you're not naturally skinny like Amber. You need to watch what you eat. You can't afford to let the weight creep on if you want to be a top gymnast, can you?'

I don't answer. There's no point. Mum can win these arguments hands down. She conjures them up from nothing, breathes life into them, nurtures them to a triumphant conclusion and then moves on speedily to the next topic of concern, and it's impossible to stop the momentum.

I don't want to upset her anyway. Which is exactly

what I would do if I dared to say, 'Actually, no one's ever asked me if I *do* want to be a top gymnast.' I hate it when she's upset, properly upset I mean, when she gets in a state. So I keep quiet and start scanning through the itinerary for tomorrow with my feet comfortably up on the dashboard.

Second mistake. 'Eva! You've torn your tracksuit bottoms! I bet you pulled them on over your trainers. How many times do I have to tell you?'

'Sorry.' No point in lying about this, she's not stupid. A deep, heartfelt sigh escapes from her. My heart sinks. I've done it again. There's no doubt about it, I'm a huge trial to her.

At home I go upstairs to take a shower before supper. Heavy rock's belting from Zac's room where he's practising his air guitar bare-chested with a towel round his waist, just out of the shower. I go to grab it but he sees it coming and jumps back, kicking the door shut in my face. I love you too, Zac.

There's no sound from the loft where Ben hangs out, so he must still be at training. He's going up to Oxford University in the autumn, my big brother, to study physics and he's got a scholarship just because he's good at rugby and they want him to play for the university. Jammy or what? Dad's over the moon. Ben's going to his old college and it's a big deal for him.

When I go past Amber's room, I glance in through the half-open door automatically. My sister's bedroom is immaculate as usual: pink throw neatly folded across the purple bedspread, fluffy cushions and soft toys scattered artlessly over the pillows, books and CDs tidily arranged on the shelves.

My room looks as if a bomb's hit it. I grab the towel I dropped on the floor last night after gym and head for the shower. I forgot, Zac has beaten me to it. It's steamy and an upended shower gel bottle is leaking its sticky contents on to the shower tray; the towels are even damper than the one I'm carrying and, most gross of all, I can see a number of Zac's dark-brown hairs clinging to the tiled walls. Time to use Mum and Dad's en suite, methinks. I nip in quick before anyone notices. What the eye doesn't see, the heart doesn't grieve over, that's my philosophy.

There's been enough grief in this family.

Dad's home. His suit is hanging up on the wardrobe door and the shirt he wore to work today is protruding from the dirty washing-basket in the bathroom. He's 'something in the City' and I'm not sure what that *something* is, except that it's to do with investments, unit trusts, stocks and shares and all sorts of other dull-sounding, soul-destroying things. What I *am* sure of is, *he* thinks it's boring too, because every day, when he comes home from work, he kind of creeps in looking wary and wearisome and the first thing he does is strip off, like he's a snake sloughing off a second skin that's too tight and restricting. Then he goes for a run in his shorts and T-shirt and when he comes back he looks fresh and alert and invigorated, more leonine now (like a lion, or a panther, in his case) than ophidion (snake-like).

I love words. I like collecting new ones but, even better, nowadays I'm becoming much more aware of how they fit together. They can be really powerful, you know. Like, it's not so much what you say, it's *how* you say it. Maybe one day I'll become a writer. Or a politician. Someone people will listen to and take notice of.

Mum wants me to be a doctor. Someone who listens to others then mends them. Only I'm no good at mending things. I'm more the type of person who breaks things up. I'm good at that.

Like Rommy and Sophie for instance. They were best friends for years, right since the start of their primary school. I got to know them when we all started at Portland High together in Year 7, all fresh from our feeder primaries and looking eagerly around to find all the new friends our mums had promised us we'd make. They were sitting in front of Hannah and me and I noticed Rommy straight away because she had a really long plait right down her back, which she could almost sit on. I've persuaded her to have it cut now and she wears it in a ponytail like the rest of us. In fact, mine's the longest now.

When I found out her name I was soooo jealous. Romilly. It sounds really pretty, not like Eva. I hate my name, it's so old-fashioned, I mean NO ONE'S called Eva nowadays. I was named after my gran, Mum's mother, who died just before I was born. It's not fair, why couldn't Dad have chosen it? He got to choose Amber which is cool.

Anyway, it wasn't long before I realized that out of all the girls in my class (I didn't bother to inspect the boys, I had enough of those at home) it was Rommy I wanted to be best friends with. She was funny and easy to get on with, one of those people who's always happy and who'll fit in with what you want to do. Everyone liked her but she was Sophie's mate.

It wasn't difficult to wriggle my way in though. I invited her home for tea a few times and she got on really well with everyone, especially Zac who probably fancies her. (She definitely fancies him; she never stops going on about him.) Mum was a bit funny at first because Rommy lives in the council flats at the other end of town but even she liked her, you can't help it.

Anyway, after a while she started coming to gym club with me (I've been going since I was five!) and she got to really like it. She's never going to be as good as me because she started too late, but she's good enough now to be in the same team. Soon we were spending all our time out of school together and Sophie didn't get a look-in, even though she joined the gym club too (spurred on by Rommy who was feeling a bit mean for neglecting her). I didn't worry about Hannah, I mean everyone needs to find their own friends, don't they?

In the end, it all worked out OK, because Hannah was already at gym club anyway; we'd both been doing it since the year dot, only I'm better than her. Soon we were all in the same competition team along with a few others in our age group from other schools. Now we do all our training together as well as go round in a group at school and everyone knows us, Rommy and me, Hannah and Sophie, as the Jimmies. And I really like this name because my surname is Jamieson so I feel as if it's my gang, named after me, which it is in a way.

Only now, Rommy and I are best friends. I make sure of that. Oh. And everyone calls her Rommy now, not Romilly.

I make sure of that too.

'Eva! Supper's on the table!'

I towel my hair roughly, run a comb through it and pull on my pyjamas. Early night tonight!

Downstairs, everyone's sitting round the kitchen table

with plates of lasagne in front of them. Ben's come in from training and is talking rugby to Dad at one end of the table. Mum's at the other end, pouring glasses of water. Zac's sitting impatiently the other side of Dad, his face a picture of torture as his plate of food steams provocatively in front of him. I slip into the chair next to Mum.

'Sorry.'

'Right, now we're all here, we can start,' says Mum reprovingly, holding a basket in front of me. 'Garlic bread?' I help myself to two slices.

'One's enough, Eva,' Mum says quietly. I put one back and start eating supper.

Opposite me, Amber's chair stands empty.

As usual, I took ages falling asleep; my brain has a fault in its off-switch. When I do eventually drop off, I have that dream again. I've had it for years. Actually, I have a number of recurring dreams but this is the one where I'm running, but it's like my legs are sticking in a gluey substance and I can't go fast enough. I don't know whether I'm chasing something or something is chasing me, but I must go faster so I turn round and run backwards and that's a bit better, though I have to keep looking over my shoulder to watch where I'm going in case I trip up. When I wake up I feel exhausted, right down to my bones, as if I really have been running all night.

I'd love to know what I'm running towards.

Or away from.

'You're awake already? Good girl.' Mum comes in with a cup of tea, bright and breezy, and swishes my curtains back. She loves competition days. 'It's a lovely day for it.'

'Lovely day for being stuck inside a gym for hours,' I grumble, not being at my best in the mornings on account of being a rubbish sleeper. I reach for the tea. 'Thanks, Mum.'

'I thought you loved gym?' says Mum, sitting down on the bed, her brow creasing into that familiar worried frown.

'Of course I do,' I say hastily, slurping my tea. 'Ow! That's hot! I'm just grumpy because I didn't sleep well.'

'Nerves,' she says, patting my arm. 'Understandable. But you've got nothing to worry about, Eva. You're the best in your age group.'

'Maybe I'm not, any more,' I say worriedly. 'Now I'm 13 plus, I'll be competing against the year above for the first time.' It's not fair the way they suddenly make the age group spread over two years. I suppose it's because it's only the good ones left by this stage. All the little wannabes have fallen by the wayside.

'There's no one there you can't beat,' Mum says consolingly, pushing back my fringe. 'You'll be fine.'

I smile and put my arms round her and give her a hug. She's right, there's no real opposition to worry about. Suddenly, I don't feel nervous at all. Mum's confidence rubs off on me and I know I'm going to win. She's great on competition days, she loves to see me performing and winning medals and cups. I've got nearly as many as Amber now, I'm catching up. They're all on display in the hall cabinet alongside Ben's rugby trophies, Zac's football awards and Dad's marathon medals. The only one who doesn't have any of her own is Mum.

Once, when we were polishing the things from the cabinet together, I said to her, 'Where are your medals then, Mum?' and she laughed and said, 'When would I have time to win medals, ferrying you lot about all day?' But then her face fell and she added, 'Anyway, you children were my trophies,' in a choked voice and she started crying.

Dad said, 'Now, what have you done to upset her?' and I said, 'Nothing!' because I really hadn't. But it must have been something serious, because she had one of her turns and went to bed for a week. And I honestly didn't mean to; I know sometimes I can be mean to people on purpose, but I never want to hurt Mum, I just want to keep her happy.

Which is why I like competition days, because she's always proud of me then. I breathe in deeply while I hug her, savouring her familiar smell of soap, fresh air and . . . I don't know . . . Mum. She pats me on the back and rocks me gently for a second, just like she did when I was little, then pulls away and holds me at arms' length and fixes me seriously with her hazel eyes, the same colour as Amber's.

'Just do your best, Eva.'

'I will, Mum.'

'I know you will.' She stands up. 'Breakfast!'

I manage to force down some cereal though I don't really feel like it, but I know I'll start feeling sick later if I've got nothing in my stomach. Mum smiles approvingly. 'Good girl, Eva. Keep up your carbs. Slow-release energy, just the ticket.' I reckon she could write a book called *The Lorna Jamieson Guide to Bringing Up the Sporty Child*, because what my mother doesn't know about nutrition and training is nobody's business.

I lapse into a daydream as Mum makes a start braiding my hair. The combing and tugging on my scalp as she separates the hair into partings is soothing and hypnotic, taking me back over years of competition days. Maybe Mum's thorough approach is the reason why we've all been so successful in our chosen sporting fields, not that Ben and Zac pay her much attention.

But we girls had the full benefit of her guiding hand from the moment Amber first tumbled her seven-year-old way into the county record books in her first gym competition amidst gasps of admiration and delight from her enthralled audience.

And I remember wanting *so* much to go out on that

floor so that everyone would smile and clap me too, but Mum kept a firm hold on my eager, wriggling body and wouldn't let me join Amber as she held her arms up high in triumph to her adoring, cheering crowd. No matter how loudly I protested, I had to endure eons of training sessions and endless competitions from the sidelines while Amber moved on gracefully from strength to strength before I was finally allowed to join gym club at the grand old age of five. And by that time, Amber was so amazingly good I despaired of ever catching her up.

But I have now. Almost.

Even though (and I would never admit this to anyone) I know deep down, I'll never be as good as Amber. Because *her* talent's the kind that's natural and awesome and only granted by the gods to the lucky, rare few. Whereas mine is the result of years of sheer, bloody-minded hard work and dedication and a touch of healthy athletic ability.

I know I'm not as good as people think I am and I've always been scared they'll find out. But I should be safe now. I mean, as far as I know, there's no one around to beat me in my age group. I'm the best in the county, I've walked away with the individual gold for the past two years.

But I still can't help feeling a fraud.

'That'll do.' Mum puts the final touches to my hair and

blasts it with some glitter spray. 'Ready, Eva? We'd better get a move on.'

'Yep.' I snap out of my thoughts. 'I said we'd pick Rommy up on the way.'

Mum tuts her disapproval. 'Why didn't you tell me before? We'll be late now.'

'No we won't!' I glance at the clock. 'We've got loads of time.'

'We don't know what the traffic will be like. Saturday morning . . .' Mum starts fretting. 'Why can't her own mother take her? Surely she's going to watch her compete?'

'She works on a Saturday.'

Mum's tongue clicks in disapproval. 'Fancy not bothering to go and watch your own child in a county competition.'

Zac looks up from the end of the table where he's trowelling his third bowl of cereal down his throat. Unbelievably, he joins in the conversation.

'Rommy's mum works weekends in a supermarket while her stepdad looks after the kids. She can't take time off when she feels like it.'

'*I* never missed a gym competition, not once, not for Amber or Eva,' Mum remarks pensively. She's just stating a fact, but it sounds a bit pious. Zac must have thought so too because he pauses before he ladles another spoonful into his mouth.

'That's different. Rommy's mum would lose her job if she didn't go in.'

Mum and I stare at Zac in surprise, Mum because he's actually given an opinion for once in his life, me because I'm wondering how come he knows so much about Rommy's family.

'You'll be late,' he points out mildly and scoops more breakfast down his gullet. 'Good luck!' he adds indistinctly, through a mouthful of cornflakes.

Rommy is waiting at the end of her road, hopping up and down with impatience. 'Your hair looks nice,' I say, turning round to inspect it as she scrambles into the back of the car. It's caught up in a high ponytail and secured in an enormous scrunchie. Mum glances at Rommy in the mirror and I notice her lips pursing fractionally and I know what she's thinking but thankfully she says nothing. It's showy but not very practical; it'll get in the way of her headstand for a start. But that's her problem, not mine. Mum's done mine in tiny French plaits, close to my head, threaded with blue and yellow ribbons, club colours. It's neat and unobtrusive.

'I'm soooo nervous,' Rommy bleats. 'What if I forget my routine again?'

'You won't,' I say quickly as Mum darts her a venomous look. 'You'll be fine.'

We get to the leisure centre with bags of time to spare. The car park is awash with neat, athletic-looking girls in hoodies and trackie pants, ranging from about nine to sixteen. Except for the tiddlers, I recognize most of them from years of competitions. Suddenly it strikes me for the first time how alike we all look. Slim ponytailed clones of each other.

At least I'm a *bit* different. My hair's in plaits.

As we get out of the car, I suddenly spy a girl who's *very* different. She stands out from the crowd. I've never seen her before. She's peering anxiously at a handout and looking around as if she's wondering where to go and I notice her because she's so big compared to the rest of the milling gymnasts. It's not so much that she's tall: she is, but not much taller than me or some of the others. It's more that she's BIG in a heavy, lumpy sort of way. Rommy's spotted her too.

'Who's *she*?'

'Never seen her before.'

The girl looks up and sees us watching her. Her face breaks into a shy smile and she hoists her bag over her shoulder.

'Watch it, she's coming this way,' I mutter.

She's wearing a tracksuit and trainers and has mousy hair scraped back into a band. There's an expression of eager friendliness on her face.

'She can't be competing!' says Rommy out of the side of her mouth, then fixes a smile on her face as the girl stops in front of us.

'Hi, I'm Patrice. Can you show me where to go? I'm new here.'

'Are you in the competition?' asks Rommy in disbelief. The girl nods eagerly.

'My first Intermediate. I'm so nervous!'

'What age-group are you in?'

'13 plus.'

'Like us. How come we haven't seen you before?' I ask curiously.

'I've just moved here. I haven't been doing gym very long. I started it to see if I could lose weight.'

Rommy eyes her doubtfully. She's obviously thinking the same as me, didn't work then, but she's too kind to say so. I struggle not to laugh. Mum takes charge and smiles at her warmly. 'You go along with Eva and Romilly, they'll show you where to go.'

Thanks, Mum. 'What did you say your name was?' I ask, as we turn to go into the centre.

'Patrice.' She stresses the second syllable, Pat*rees*, but then she adds, 'Call me Patty, everyone does.'

I nod, biting my lip, trying to suppress a giggle. She continues, 'I like your name, Romilly, that's really pretty.'

'*She's* Romilly,' I say curtly. 'I'm Eva.'

'Eva?' She considers for a moment, trying it out. 'That's unusual.'

Not as unusual as yours, I think grimly, linking my arm through Rommy's and whispering in her ear. Rommy bursts out laughing, then stops immediately with a guilty look at Patty. When I glance at her, the new girl's face is tinged pink and her eyes are cast down.

But it's not my fault the new girl's got super-sensitive hearing. She wasn't supposed to hear what I called her.

Anyway, looking like that, she must be used to it by now.

Fatty Patty doesn't look so eager to please any more.

I feel a bit mean though. Trust me, I've done it again. Now I'll have to make it up to her.

The story of my life.

Inside the sports hall, it's heaving. All five gym clubs are present today, represented by girls from all over the county. Hannah and Sophie are there already, adding the finishing touches to their appearance. Sophie has sprayed sparkles all over her face, neck and shoulders. Mike eyes her disapprovingly.

'Is that really necessary?' he asks. Sophie looks suitably repentant but once he's moved away, she pulls a face.

'Needn't have bothered anyway,' she pouts. 'The boys are not on till tomorrow.'

Hannah and I roll our eyes at each other. We've been doing gym for ages and we just don't get Sophie's attitude. She could be good if she took it more seriously, even though she started quite late.

Actually, though I make out I disapprove, I'm secretly glad she's a bit slack, it means I don't have to keep an eye on her too much. In fact, I reckon the only reason she's kept on coming for the past two years is because we train with the boys a couple of times a week (well, not with them exactly; they're there at the same time as we are but they do their own stuff). She's got a thing about Jason, who's our top male gymnast, but she needn't bother; he's way out of her league and he's only interested in his sport. Not having brothers, she has no idea how single-minded the average male is.

Talking of brothers . . . 'Is Zac coming to cheer you on?' asks Rommy innocently.

She doesn't fool me or anyone else.

I snort derisively. 'Like, why would he?'

She colours up and mutters, 'I just wondered . . .'

Hannah, who never misses a chance to score points against Rommy since she was ousted from my number one slot, chants, 'Romm-ee for Za-ac! Romm-ee for Za-ac!'

Rommy squeals in protest, her face on fire, and Hannah and Sophie collapse into fits of giggles. My skin prickles with irritation. I'm not too sure about this, my brother and my best friend. I was hoping it was just in Rommy's dreams, but after Zac's little outburst this morning, I'm starting to wonder. I'd rather they kept their distance, to be honest. I mean, *I'm* supposed to be the most important person in Rommy's life and as for Zac, well he's never been that interested in me so why should he suddenly be so fascinated by my best mate?

'I think he's got a date,' I lie and have the satisfaction of seeing her face fall.

'Zac?' says Mum, who appears behind me from nowhere. 'What, with a football? Come on, girls, you need to warm up.'

Peeved, I follow Mum on to the floor. Rommy dances along behind me, perky again.

Mum used to be an assistant coach at gym club. She did a course when Amber started, thinking it would be good if she could help her with her moves. I don't know how she coped in those days, looking after us lot, doing coaching courses, helping at the gym. She's let her certification lapse now, but today Mike's asked her to do a warm-up with us because he's officiating.

She knows her stuff and puts us through our paces, then gives us time at the end to run through our floor routines. My irritation disappears as I become absorbed in my moves. No surprises today, I've done all these before. I'm going for the safe bet in this competition, my routine a tried and tested mixture of leaps, flicks and tumbles and some zany dance steps, nothing too difficult but guaranteed to bring me a relatively high score. I can relax and enjoy this one. Out of the corner of my eye I see the new girl hurling herself around the floor, but I'm concentrating too hard to see what she's got in her routine. Not a lot, I guess.

I say I can relax today but in actual fact I know I won't really let up till that gold medal is placed around my neck. Then I'll step forward and salute the crowd with my arms in the air and bask in the glow of Mike's approval and the pride shining from Mum's face. And it will all be worth it.

Soon it's time for the competition to begin. The music starts and the audience picks up the rhythm and claps. We all process into the hall and march around the perimeter of the floor to the beat, backs straight, chins up, hair so tightly tied back our scalps tingle, fingers and toes pointing. I love this bit. The littlies bristle with anticipation, one or two rigid with nerves, but most beaming with excitement and waving to their mums and dads. Sometimes I recognize my younger self among the more serious of them, in a bullish tilt of a chin or a grim determination round the mouth.

Today, one little girl reminds me of Amber, something about the graceful turn of her long neck and a jauntiness of step. I glance at Mum as I march past and she's not looking at me, she's staring straight at her, so I know she feels it too.

The march finishes and we take our places at the edge of the mats, the Jimmies all in a line together. Parents edge forward on their benches, craning to spot their daughters and size up the opposition. A cloud of anxiety hovers over them as they exchange urgent whispered asides and hiss their younger offspring into silence. It's time to begin. The first competitor walks out on to the floor and takes up a pose, ready to start, and a hush settles on the audience. She looks doll-like, unreal, an ornamental figurine of a gymnast. Her music starts and she springs into life.

As each of the younger age groups take their turn, I sit between Hannah and Rommy, glued to the dramas unfolding before us, conscious that what looks seemingly fluid and effortless to the untrained eye is actually the result of months of arduous preparation and contains scores of tiny (or sometimes glaring!) faults. And I wonder how many times over the years Mum's sat here like this, first supporting Amber, then waiting for my turn, and I turn to look at her.

She's rapt, her lips minutely opening and closing, mouthing the moves she knows by heart. As one tiny competitor manages to pull off a round-off flick and beams triumphantly, Mum claps exuberantly and turns to look at me, her face lit up. I grin back, enjoying sharing the moment with her, and join in the applause, feeling warm inside. This is why I love competition days. They make all the hours of tiring, punishing, boring, mind-numbing, back-breaking training worth it, if they can bring back that smile on Mum's face.

And when I take that gold medal home at the end of the day, I'll give it to Mum to place in the cabinet and it'll make her happy, won't it?

It'll make up for the fact that Amber won't bring them home any more.

The littlies finish, then it's time for a break and a second warm-up and then we're on. Sophie's on the floor first and I yell, 'Go, Sophie!' as she walks over to take up her position on the mat. The rest of the Jimmies join in and she looks back at us and giggles. Mike frowns.

It's so easy, you know, to break her concentration.

Still, she manages to produce a nice, neat little routine nevertheless. She's better than I thought.

Hannah's next and I cheer her on to the floor too; no ulterior motive here, she's no competition. Poor Hannah, she produces her usual solid performance but she lacks the wow factor and gets perfunctory applause. I catch sight of her face as she walks off the floor and she's looking downcast so I yell, 'Well done, Hannah!' and cheer, and people in the audience glance at me and smile, probably thinking, 'What a nice girl!' and clap a bit harder. If they only knew. I can afford to be generous here, she's not going to come anywhere near my score.

No one else from the other teams gives me anything

to worry about, not even in the year above me, and I feel more and more relaxed. Soon it's my turn.

I walk on to the floor to the sound of wild whoops and admonitions to 'Go, Eva!' – one of the pay-offs for cheering everyone else on. The difference is, it doesn't intimidate me, I thrive on attention. I take my place at the corner of the mat, right leg pointed, arms stretched above my head, waiting still as a statue for the music to start. Two bars in and I bounce into action, in a chain of tumbles I've done many times before. My routine is light and simple, a series of stands, rolls, walkovers and somersaults linked by a nice lively dance number that soon has the crowd clapping to the beat. They lift my performance and I fly through it.

At the end I hold my position to a round of appreciative applause then salute to the judges and turn to look at Mum. It's OK: her smile is modest but I can tell from the way she's clapping, arms raised high above her head, that she's pleased with my performance. I grin at her happily as I sit down cross-legged to watch the others.

Mum was right, I'm far and away the best in my age group, there's no one to touch me. Not even Sophie. When it's Rommy's turn she starts off well but then she messes up again. Just as she's about to launch herself into a tumble she hesitates, as if she thinks she might have

29

gone wrong in her routine. She recovers but it throws her out of her stride and her somersaults are flat, costing her valuable marks.

She's lost her nerve.

Never mind, it's an individual competition. This time she's not going to lose us a team medal. As she comes off the floor I cheer, 'Romm-ee! Romm-ee!' and give her a hug, but she's close to tears and sits down forlornly on the floor. I put an arm round her and consult my programme. Just one more to go, P. Williams.

It's the clueless Patty. She lumbers on to the floor, looking extremely self-conscious (so she should!), and takes up position as if she's waiting for a bus, bum pushed out at a most unbecoming angle. I dig Rommy in the ribs with a grin. 'This should be good!'

The music starts. 'Not "The Entertainer" again!' I groan. Patty stretches as if she's suddenly woken up to the fact that the bus is coming, then spins into action with a jump, full-turn. 'Ooooh, wobbly flesh!' I giggle but then my jaw falls as Fatty Patty lifts up on to her toes and launches herself into a round-off flick, followed by a tuck-back somersault.

'Not bad,' gasps Rommy in surprise. I watch as Patty chassés across the floor, surprisingly light on her feet. The crowd pick up the beat and start clapping her along as she does a body-wave (dear me, all that rippling flesh) then bursts into applause as she executes a series of high leaps.

'They're not supposed to do that! They're supposed to wait till the end!' I hiss, glaring balefully at the audience, but they're oblivious. All eyes are glued on Patty, the human diplodocus, as she takes to the air. Beside me, Rommy breathes, 'She's good!' as four tons of female flesh hurls itself into an aerial cartwheel. More fancy dance steps follow culminating with an over-ambitious but nonetheless impressive attempt at an Arabian somi and Patty Williams finally collapses back into waiting-for-bus mode, chest heaving, sweat pouring off in buckets.

And the crowd goes wild.

When I get home that night, Amber's waiting for me in her bedroom.

'Where've you been?' I ask crossly.

'Around.' She's painting her toenails, a lurid pink I recognize immediately.

'That's mine!' I snatch it off her. 'You've been in my room again.'

'Tell Mum then,' she laughs. 'By the way, congratulations. Another one for the cabinet.'

'Were you there?' I ask, startled. She points at the medal hanging round my neck and says, 'Duh!' Then she adds, quite considerately for Amber, 'How did it go then?'

I touch the gold medal thoughtfully. 'OK.' I was a clear winner, my vault strong and controlled, my combined scores making me way ahead of Sophie, who came second and Hannah who'd come third. A clean sweep for the Jimmies, a cause for celebration, even though

Rommy's flat tumbles had cheated her of a place in the medals. Mike had been well pleased with us.

'Swept the board!' he'd gloated. 'Well done, girls. Especially you, Eva,' he'd added, singling me out for special praise and giving me, literally, a pat on the back. I'd felt myself swelling with pride, especially when he'd turned to Mum and said, 'Sound as a board. You can always rely on Eva,' and Mum had smiled with pleasure and given me a hug. I'd thought I'd burst with happiness.

But then he'd spoilt it because he'd added, 'Did you see that new girl? Where's she come from?' and Mum had answered, 'I don't know, but she's good, isn't she?'

'Where did she come in the contest?' I'd asked.

Mike had gone off to find out and when he came back he was shaking his head. 'Eighth,' he said in disgust. 'Purists.'

A warm feeling of relief had flooded me. 'Not so good then, after all,' I'd crowed from the safe position of gold medallist.

Mike frowned at me.

'Don't you believe it,' he said. 'That girl's a natural, take my word.'

It still rankled. In some stupid way I felt as if Patty Williams had stolen my thunder. Amber, being Amber, is on to it immediately.

'So, what's with the face?'

I sigh. Her purple bedspread is smooth to the touch. I run my hand over it, savouring its cool silkiness. It reminds me of the blanket I had on my bed when I was little. I hated my cot. I can actually remember the bars and the horror of being trapped behind them. Mum delayed putting me in a bed because I'd been such a nightmare sleeper; she thought I'd get out and be running around all night.

But when at last I went into my new bed I had a new blanket. It was soft and white and woolly, and it had a satin band on the top, and I loved it. I used to stroke that band every night. Much to Mum and Dad's amazement, once I had one thumb crammed in my mouth, my index finger curled round my nose and the other hand clutching and caressing that cool, smooth glossiness, I'd give in at last and go to sleep.

My Piece of Cold, I used to call it. It was the most soothing thing in the world. I had it for years. I've no idea where it went to, it just disappeared one day. I cried my head off and everyone searched high and low but we couldn't find it anywhere.

'What's the matter, Evie?' Amber persisted.

'Nothing. Nothing's the matter.'

Her fingertips brush my cheek, light as a feather. 'Doesn't look like nothing to me. Who's upset my little sister? Tell Amber.'

I raise my eyes and look at her. You wouldn't think there was nearly four years between us any more. I'm as big as her now and we look alike, though her blonde hair is piled in a wild heap on top of her head with wavy tendrils escaping sexily round her face while mine is tamed primly into a crossword puzzle of tiny French plaits. Her tone is gentle but her eyes are cool and challenging.

She's fearless, Amber, always has been. She wouldn't be afraid of a stupid, lumpy new girl who came eighth to her first.

'Eva? Zac? Everybody!' Mum's voice floats up from downstairs. 'Supper's ready. Where are you?'

I jump up and slip out quickly. Too late. Mum's already halfway up the stairs when I come out of the door. She stops in her tracks.

'What are you doing in Amber's room?' Her face softens. 'You've been telling her about your medal, haven't you?'

Zac appears out of his bedroom, rubbing his eyes. He's still in his PJ bottoms and looks as if he's been asleep all day. Mum's attention turns to him.

'Haven't you got dressed today?'

'Yeah! I've been playing football.'

'In your pyjamas?' I ask sweetly and snap his elastic as we go downstairs.

'Gerroff!' he growls, then, 'How did you get on?'

'Duh!' I say, echoing Amber and hold the medal out from my neck, as far as the ribbon will let me.

'Well done.'

I count the seconds. One, two three, four . . . then . . . 'How did Romilly do?' he asks innocently.

'Unplaced,' I say shortly.

'No! Did she go wrong on the floor again? She was worried about that? Is she upset?'

'Zac! Why this sudden rush of interest? All I got was a "Well done".' I feel righteously peeved. Then I catch sight of his crestfallen face and relent. 'Ask her yourself,' I say and chuck my phone at him.

'I can't do that,' he says, looking horrified, his face pink with embarrassment.

'Why not? Put her out of her misery, she's dying to get her clutches into you.'

'How do you know?' His face is a picture, like an eager sheep.

'How do I know?' I give what I hope is an ironic laugh, then adopt a falsetto voice. 'Is Zac coming to watch you today, Eva? Is Zac playing football? Is Zac going out with anyone? Is Zac still breathing? Zac, Zac, Zac; Yak, Yackety-Yaaak!' My voice rises into a squawk and I flap my elbows like wings. Despite himself, Zac laughs.

'Well, if you're sure . . .'

'She's mad as a chicken about you, Zac. And you can't make her feel worse than she's already feeling.'

'Thanks, Eva. I owe you one.' Zac pockets my phone as we go in to supper and treats me to a full-beam grin that lights up his normal caveman-like expression. Just for a minute I have a glimmer of understanding what Rommy sees in my Neanderthal brother. He looks nice when he smiles. I guess we all do.

I'm just not used to being the one putting a smile on his face.

At school on Monday, I wish I hadn't bothered. When we hang out at breaktime, Rommy prattles on non-stop about 'Zac said this' and 'Zac said that' until we're all sick of the sound of her voice. This is the result of just one phone call. They haven't even arranged to meet up yet; goodness knows what they'll be like when they do.

'You'll be glued at the hip like Daronica,' Hannah says, pointing to the resident lovebirds of Year 9, Darren and Veronica, who have become so inseparable they've merged identities as far as we're concerned, so we just refer to them by one joint name.

'*And* you'll be as boring as Alice,' I yawn, nodding towards our class genius who's continuing a fascinating (not!) discussion on greenhouse gases we've just had in geography with her trusty band of nerds. Actually, I'm

37

secretly in awe of her because she's brilliant at everything, but no one would ever know. I cover it up with a very healthy dose of scorn, which she frequently wilts under.

'*And* you'll get frumpy-looking because you won't bother trying any more,' chips in Sophie, who's jealous as hell because she's not getting anywhere with Jason and who is a tad too much in touch with her inner high-street diva.

Rommy ignores us all and launches into a long catalogue of what Zac likes to eat. I could have saved her the bother, I've seen everything he's gulped down his gullet for the past thirteen years, at much closer quarters than I would have wished. How romantic is that, to tell each other what you like to stuff your face with? It's a pack of lies anyway, he's never had tofu or falafels in his life. From choice he'd live on giant-sized boxes of cornflakes and Big Macs.

I'm wondering how much more of this I can stand and wishing passionately that I hadn't given in to the weirdly nice Eva that sometimes bobs up from deep inside me in a weak moment and given him Rommy's phone number in the first place, when suddenly her face changes and she squeals, 'Look! It's her! Look! Whatsername!'

I turn round to see what she's gawping at that could possibly be more fascinating than my boring brother.

And I gasp aloud.

It's Fatty Patty.

She's walking down the corridor towards us with Mr Smith, our deputy head, and she's wearing our school uniform and looking like a sack of potatoes. Her eyes light up when she sees us. (Ha ha, eyes, potatoes, get it?) I wish I could pass on this gem to the others but it's too late. Mr Smith and the sack of spuds stop before us.

'Aah, here we are,' he booms. 'Eva, Sophie, um Romilly and . . .?'

'Hannah?'

'That's it. This is Patrice. She's joining us in Year 9 and she says she knows you already.'

'The Jimmies,' breathes Patty, her moon-face beaming down at us.

I glare back at her and a cloud passes over the moon, dimming its beam. Mr Smith doesn't notice.

'Well, I'll leave her in your capable hands. She's going to be in your form. Patrice tells me she's a gymnast, like you.'

'Does she now?' I mutter.

Hannah's staring at her with interest. 'You were at the competition on Saturday!'

Well done, Hannah. Slow on the uptake, but you get there in the end.

Patty nods eagerly. 'Yes. I saw you too. You were sooo good. You got a medal, didn't you?'

'Bronze,' says Hannah, flattered. 'Sophie got the silver . . .'

'Wow!' breathes Patty, as if she'd been awarded the Victoria Cross. 'Well done.'

Sophie smiles modestly back at her. 'Thanks.'

'. . . and Eva got the gold.'

Patty turns to me, a look of adulation on her face. I jump in quick before she starts oozing all over me.

'Are you stalking us?'

Patty looks momentarily stunned then giggles nervously. 'No, I've just moved here. Mr Smith gave me a class list and your photos were on it and I recognized you immediately. You all did so well at the competition on Saturday and everyone was talking about you. You're the Jimmies, aren't you?'

'That's us.' I decide my nails deserve more attention than she does and an uneasy silence falls.

After a while, Patty says in a quiet, polite voice, 'I hope you don't mind me saying I knew you to Mr Smith?'

Everyone waits for me to say something. The trouble is, I've discovered a cuticle that needs pushing back urgently.

Rommy stirs uncomfortably. 'We don't mind.'

The silence grows. I carry on examining my nails.

'*Do* we, Eva?' she says pointedly.

I glance up. 'Do we *what*?' I say in my best bored-sounding voice.

Rommy frowns. OK, I know I'm acting like a D-list celeb on a bad day but I can't help it. It can take just one little thing to come up behind me unnoticed and push me into a deep, dark hole. A hole that is easy to fall into, but hard to climb out of.

But this time it's not just one little thing. It's a ginormous monster called Patty Williams.

The gigantoraptor is invading my life.

A gigantoraptor, for the uninitiated, is a new feathered breed of dinosaur. Well, it's not new, obviously, it's eighty-five million years old, but it's only recently been discovered and given a name. Anyway, the crucial point is, it's not only enormous, even by gigantic ancient lizard standards, weighing 1.4 tons, but it's feathered and presumably it flies, because it's a 'raptor' which means it's a bird, not a 'saurus' which is a lizard.

Sorry, I told you I loved words.

They should have called it a Pattyraptor. She's enormous.

And she flies. Unfortunately.

The gigantoraptor was a bird of prey. The top of the food chain. Naturally. Nothing was going to attack that humungous chickadee. Every other fledgling was in awe of it.

Amber wouldn't be. She wouldn't be scared of an

overweight bird. I can hear her voice now.

'Get a grip, Eva, you shivering wreck. The world's moved on and now the Evasaurus has precedence.'

Yeah, she's right. I'm not afraid of you, Pattyraptor, or anyone else for that matter. You see, unlike you, I've got my feet planted firmly on the ground. So just don't try to soar too high, Big Bird, or the Evasaurus will bring you crashing back down.

When the bell goes I march off to science ahead of the others. I don't want Patty Williams hanging around the Jimmies. That remark about her stalking us was only half-joking. When we line up outside the science lab I can see that Rommy's still way back down the corridor, checking Fat Pat's timetable with her. Trust Rommy, she's always a soft touch.

When they finally catch up with us, Patty's grinning like a Cheshire cat behind her. What's she got to look so happy about? I make room for Rommy against the wall. Then, as Patty tries to squeeze in beside her, I raise my eyebrows.

'Excuse me? Pushing in or what?'

'Eva!' gasps Rommy.

Patty flushes and the Cheshire grin drops off her face. 'Sorry,' she mumbles and moves away to the end of the queue. I feel a bit mean. I'd expected a bit more resistance than that.

The lab door opens and Mr Gee barks, 'Come in quietly!'

There's nothing I can do now. Rommy's staring at me as if I've shot my own grandmother. I shrug my shoulders. 'She'll get over it.'

It's not till I've sat down in my usual place and I'm taking my file out of my bag that I realize Rommy isn't sitting beside me. She's at the front introducing Patty to Mr Gee. Patty's switched the grin on again and her eyes have disappeared into folds of flesh.

She's got over it already.

I'm soooo cross when Mr Gee says, 'Nice to meet you, Patrice. Look, sit here at the front with Romilly for the time being, then I can give you a hand if you need help.'

I'm surprised Rommy doesn't turn round and mouth 'Help!' at me. Instead she sits where she's told and opens her book and shows Patty where we're up to. The fat girl listens to her agog as if she's never heard anything so fascinating.

Which leaves me on my own. I glance around quickly so I can tell Hannah to come and sit by me, but she's already in her usual place with Sophie and the two of them are in total cahoots, probably jabbering on about how I froze the new girl out.

So I spread my stuff out so it doesn't look as if I'm a Billy-no-mates and try to concentrate on the lesson. I

44

like science and maths normally, they appeal to my logical, ordered side. You know what to expect with them. I'm a bit like Mum, I don't like surprises.

I'm not a boffin, mind. I'm no science geek. Like I said, my favourite thing is words. I like writing poems and stories; my English teacher says I'm good at conveying feelings. I could write one now, all right, about what it feels like to be sitting on your own in a science lab while your best friend's gone off with the new girl and EVERYONE else has got someone to sit by, even Smellody Melody with the personal hygiene problem who's next to Graham who spends every lesson exploring his nasal passages with his index finger and has warts all over his hands. Gross. But at least they've got each other for company.

What makes it worse is, we're doing pair work and I have to match up with Mr Gee with his dog's breath and dandruff shoulders because there's nobody else. It's soooo embarrassing! In front of me I can see Rommy and Patty with their heads together twittering away. Rommy's like that, she'd be nice to the fat girl even though she'd rather be sitting next to me.

Obviously.

The lesson drags on for ever but at last the bell goes. I can't get out of that room fast enough. I grab Rommy by the arm as I go past, yanking her up out of her seat, away from Patty who looks at me bemused.

'What's the hurry?' Rommy asks, bewildered, as I march her into the canteen, my arm through hers.

'Thought you'd be glad to get away from the Blob.'

'The blo— D'you mean Patty?'

'Absolutely. You poor thing. I nearly died when old Gee put you with her. What a pain!' I study the chilled cabinet in front of us. 'What d'you fancy today? Sausage and pickle sarnies? Or something hot?'

'No thanks.' Rommy's voice is quiet. 'I want a salad.'

'You sickening for something?' I glance at her. Her face is expressionless. 'Watching your weight?' I tease, poking her in the ribs. As if! Rommy's got a lovely figure, slim but curvy in the right places. I suspect that's the reason Zac is drawn to her rather than to her superior intelligence or acerbic wit. (Not that my brother is shallow!)

She frowns. 'No, I just fancy a salad that's all.' Her voice is short, irritable.

'Only joking! Think I'll join you.' I reach for a salad too, even though I really want something more substantial. Behind me, Sophie says, 'Are we getting salad?' and looks disappointed, then she and Hannah each put one on their trays. For a moment I'm dumbfounded. It hadn't really occurred to me before but now I think about it, we all tend to get the same things for lunch.

Well, I suppose we are the Jimmies.

We're all sitting at one of the bench tables tucking into our yummy (not) assortments of wilted green leaves, damp grated carrot, squashy tomatoes and grey wrinkled potatoes splattered in dubious, artificially bright-yellow mayonnaise, when I notice Patty Williams wending her way precariously across the canteen, tray piled high with hot, steaming food. I scoop a large forkful of mixed leaves into my mouth and nudge Rommy.

'Watch out, two-ton-truck alert!' I say indistinctly.

Mistake. 'Patty! Over here!' says Rommy, rising to her feet and waving. Patty comes to an emergency stop, negotiates a three-point turn with difficulty and trundles her way to our table, her lights on full beam.

'Budge up, Eva,' bosses Rommy and shoves me along the bench with her hip.

I choke on my mouthful of green stuff and grab a glass of water. Second mistake. The water gets as far as my throat, which is now packed tight with leaves and, having nowhere else to go, sprays back out.

'EVA!!!'

Everyone's looking at me. Incredibly, at this point in time I'm more concerned about trying to gulp oxygen into my starved lungs than the embarrassment factor. I never knew the simple act of breathing could be so difficult. Or so noisy. Rommy thumps me on the back but it's no good, I flail, gasping for air, like a fish caught on a hook, and feel a blind moment of panic.

Suddenly I feel a massive thud in my back and I jerk upright, then the next minute a pair of strong arms comes round me from behind and starts pumping me violently, just beneath my ribs. There is absolutely nothing I can do as I am thrashed about like a rag-doll in the arms of some demented sadist. The end is inevitable: whether it's by choking or being palpated to death seems merely academic.

Then, all of a sudden, I give an almighty belch and a wad of tightly packed green stuff, flaked with orange carrot gratings, shoots out of my mouth and lands on the table in front of me in a gross, soggy heap. I collapse back on to the bench, retching and gasping for air.

As my pulse rate returns to normal and my heart stops thudding, I look up, and my heart sinks. I realize that I and the offending vegetable matter have the undivided attention of the whole school.

I'm mortified.

Then a cheer goes up and everyone claps. People are glad I'm back from the dead. It makes me feel so popular! My embarrassment recedes and I smile modestly and wave as people yell out, 'Well done!' and 'Good on you!'

'What's her name?' I hear someone say near me and I'm surprised because I would have said everyone in the school knows me because of Ben and Zac and Amber, of course, and because everyone knows I'm a gymnast.

But apparently not, because someone else says, 'Never seen her before.'

'She must be new.' The conversation continues and suddenly I register that they're not talking about me at all, they're looking at someone behind me and I turn around.

Patty Williams, the two-ton truck, lights blazing, pats me on the shoulder. 'Are you all right now, Eva?' she asks solicitously.

'The Heimlich manoeuvre,' says the teacher on canteen duty, who, now the drama is over, materializes out of nowhere. Where was he when he was needed? 'Well done, young lady. I've never seen that done before.'

And, horror of horrors, at last I realize that:

1. Fatty Patty was the mentalist sadist.
2. She's responsible for dislodging from my airways that disgusting gloop which is now on display for the whole world to see.
3. Everyone's clapping her, not me.
And,
4. I will hate her for ever.

No one's in when I get home from school. I glance at the clock. That's strange. Mum should be pottering about in the kitchen now, making an early tea for me so I can get off to gym club. Zac's not back from school yet either. I'm dying to find out whether he witnessed that dreadful debacle at lunchtime. He's bound to have heard about it anyway.

It was soooo humiliating. I wish Mum was home. I want to tell her all about it, get it over and done with, so it stops appearing in capital letters in my mind, over and over again, like the headlines on News 24. YEAR NINE GIRL VOMITS HERSELF BACK TO LIFE IN FRONT OF WHOLE SCHOOL . . . YEAR 9 GIRL VOMITS HERSELF BACK TO LIFE IN FRONT OF WHOLE SCHOOL . . . YEAR 9 GIRL . . . Mum will put it in perspective for me then I can file it away in the special drawer in my head labelled, 'Never to be referred to again.'

There's quite a lot in that drawer.

Upstairs, Amber's door is wide open but there's no sign of her. The house feels silent, desolate. I don't want to be on my own. I climb up the loft ladder into Ben's bedroom even though I'm sure he's not there. You can tell, can't you, if a room is empty before you go into it? It's like a sixth sense. I reckon in the ancient past, like the Neanderthal era, we probably had loads of senses that we don't use any more.

I was right, Ben's not around. There are plenty of traces of *him* though: his rugby kit in a tangled heap on the floor; discarded underwear (gross); open textbooks on the desk next to an A4 pad covered in doodles and diagrams; a mug of cold coffee with a grey skin on top and a half-eaten sandwich mouldering by the bed; empty crisp packets by the overflowing bin. Why do boys need to eat so much? There's also a lingering male smell of socks and unwashed kit. Mum doesn't wander into this part of the house as much as she does into mine and Amber's bedrooms. I don't blame her.

I linger though. It's comforting feeling the presence of my big brother in this quiet, empty house. I curl up on his bed, pulling the duvet around me. He was my ally, Ben, when I was little, sticking up for me when Amber lorded it over me. This time next year, he'll be at Oxford. I'll miss him. The house will be really quiet then. I snuggle down, ignoring the faintly musky smell of the bottom sheet, and let my eyes close. All I need now is my beloved Piece of Cold.

I must have dropped off anyway because suddenly I'm getting in the back of the car with Amber and slamming the door angrily. Zac's in the front. It's THAT MORNING again and my sister and I are still squabbling. The argument has moved on now. Amber is trying to make out I was such an awful baby they tried to get rid of me.

'We put you up for adoption, you were such a nuisance,' she jeers.

I know she's making it up but my nine-year-old self can't help rising to the bait.

'That's not true, is it, Mum? You didn't want to give me away, did you?'

'Of course not, sweetheart.' Mum starts up the car and swivels round to look out of the back window, her eyes gazing past us as if we're not there.

'See?' I'm triumphant.

Amber wrinkles her nose. 'She would say that, wouldn't she? The truth is, no one would have you, so we were stuck with you.'

'Mu-um!'

Zac chuckles. Mum slips the car into reverse and

releases the handbrake. The car rolls backwards, Mum still staring behind us, watching where she's going. 'Stop teasing her, Amber, you know what a sensitive soul she is.' But her eyes are sparkling and you can tell she's trying not to laugh.

I *hate* being laughed at. I lash out with my fist at Amber and she yells, 'Mum! Eva's going mental!'

The car comes to an abrupt halt and we jerk forward. 'Stop it, the pair of you!' snaps Mum and she glares at us both. 'Now put that seat belt on, Amber.'

My sister pouts but she straps herself in. 'I've got mine on already,' I say righteously as Mum starts up the car again and we reverse out on to the main road.

'Good girl,' says Mum.

'Creep!' hisses Amber.

'Pig!' I shoot back.

'Psycho!'

'Minger!'

Amber's face contorts with fury. I smile smugly and turn away to look out of the window.

I don't know how long I've been asleep but the sound of the front door slamming wakes me and then I hear footsteps trudging heavily up the stairs. I sit bolt upright and fling the duvet back. I don't want Ben to catch me in here like some weird sort of Goldilocks, sleeping in his bed. But before my feet touch the floor, a bedroom door bangs shut and I think, phew, it must be Zac and I relax.

Until it starts. That noise again. It's a muffled but, at the same time, piercing sound, something like a cross between the wind blowing through the eaves on a stormy night and a cat yowling. It's dark and mournful and haunting and I've heard it so often over the past four years but each time it makes my blood run cold.

I hate this sound. It's the worst in the world.

It's the sound of crying and it's coming from Amber's room.

I crawl back under Ben's duvet and put my hands over my ears, curling myself up into a ball and rocking myself gently. And I stay there, blocking the noise out as much as I can till, at last, it fades away, but it's not until I hear Dad's car pulling into the drive that I actually uncurl myself from my tight, protective ball and even then, only when I hear his key in the lock and he calls, 'I'm ho-ome!' do I know it's safe to come down. I climb noiselessly down Ben's ladder and stand at the top of the stairs, watching him as he checks the post in the hallway. Dad looks up and sees me standing there in my school uniform like a silent ghost and the light goes out of his face.

'What's up?' he asks. Like he has to. I indicate with my head towards Amber's room.

He nods and makes his way upstairs slowly. 'Get changed, Eva. I'll take you to gym tonight.'

In the end I'm late. Dad is ages upstairs and when he comes down he looks exhausted.

'Is she OK?' Zac asks. He's arrived back as I'm making myself a peanut butter and jam sandwich and he can tell by my face what's happened. I make one for him too. We sit in front of the telly eating them, though neither of us is concentrating on the programme. Nor do we mention my most embarrassing school moment ever. It doesn't seem quite so important now.

'She's sleeping,' says Dad. Poor thing, he looks as if he could do with a bit of kip himself.

'Do we need to call the doctor?' I ask.

He shakes his head. 'I don't think so. A good night's sleep, that's all she needs. I'm sure she'll be fine in the morning.'

My eyes meet with Zac's. Who's he trying to kid?

'What brought it on?' Zac asks.

'Who knows?' Dad says shortly and turns away. 'Come on, Eva, let's get you to gym club.'

It's silent in the car. He's always quiet, Dad, at the best of times; it's Mum who does all the chatting normally. When I steal a peek at him I see his face is closed and his brow is wrinkled into tight frown lines.

My heart sinks. He's worried about Mum. Despite what he said, he thinks we might be in for the long haul.

You see, it wasn't Amber howling her head off in her bedroom.

It was Mum.

In case you haven't worked it out yet, Mum has funny turns where she gets really miserable. It's like life seems to become so unbearable she just ceases to function and she breaks down and cries a lot. Sometimes these episodes can be over quite quickly and she emerges the next day almost as if nothing has happened and carries on as normal, only she's a more muted version of herself for a while, if you know what I mean.

But sometimes it goes on and on. Once, about three years ago, she disappeared for a while and I thought she'd run away and left me and I cried and cried even though Dad explained to me she'd been taken into hospital. That was a really bad time. They wouldn't let me see her, only he was allowed, and I thought she'd never come back. It's not usually that bad but sometimes she's in bed for a week or two and Dad has to take time off work to look after her and we all walk round on tiptoes so we don't disturb Mum because she needs to rest.

Then the house feels strange and hushed, so I stay out of it as much as possible. I go round to Rommy's flat where her mum and stepdad have got two little kids and the telly is permanently on in the corner and, though I know Mum would disapprove, I like it there because it's noisy and full of life, though it would do my head in if I had to put up with it permanently.

I never tell Rommy about Mum's funny turns though. I don't want her feeling sorry for me. She's sort of got used to me hanging out big-time at her place sometimes (when things are bad at home with Mum), then not seeing so much of me (when things are back to normal), but she doesn't know the real reason why. She just thinks I'm moody.

I'm lucky I've got Rommy as a best mate.

I give a big sigh. Dad glances at me and his face softens. He pats my knee.

'Don't worry, babes. Mum'll be fine.'

'You reckon?'

'Of course. We've been through worse than this, haven't we?'

I nod. He smiles and his eyes crinkle momentarily then his eyebrows settle back down into a low brooding line. I'd do anything to lift them again so I take a risk and tell him the vomiting salad story in a humorous, self-deprecating way. It works. He roars with laughter.

'Could have been worse, you know. You could have wet your pants in front of the whole class.'

'Did that happen to you?' I stare at him in surprise.

He nods. 'Fourth of September, 1966. I'll never forget that date. My first day at infant school. I was so busy playing in the Wendy house I forgot to go until it was too late. The worst thing was, I had to wear a pair of girl's lacy knickers all day.' He shudders. 'The most humiliating moment ever.'

'I don't know.' My mind goes unwillingly back to the lesson preceding the vomiting salad scenario. 'What about having no one to sit by in class and having to sit by yourself? That's pretty mortifying.'

'Oh yeah,' Dad says, screwing his eyes up in pain, as if he can remember what that feels like too. 'Or how about fainting in assembly!'

'You didn't, did you?'

He nods. 'Second year of secondary school, a Wednesday morning just before Christmas. I was carried out by the head of PE.' Dad winces at the memory. 'What could be worse than that?'

'Reading aloud in class in Year 7 and pronouncing "Grand Prix" as "grand pricks" and everyone howling.' My cheeks flame as I recall the moment I realized what I'd said and saw that even my teacher was creased up laughing at me. Dad guffaws.

'Nice one! I can remember what it's like to be the only person to turn up on a charity day at school wearing school uniform . . .'

'And I can remember what it's like to be the very last person left to be picked for a side . . .'

'Ouch!' Dad looks at me sympathetically and I wish I hadn't admitted that. I don't want him to feel sorry for me, I just want to make him laugh.

'It was ages ago,' I add quickly and he chuckles and continues with the game.

'How about calling your teacher Mum by accident when you're fifteen and nearly six foot tall and everyone laughs at you!'

'Or sitting on some chocolate when you're wearing white jeans!'

'Or farting in class . . .'

'Da-ad!'

'It was an accident!'

'Yeah, right!'

He's laughing now, we both are, fit to burst. Then, as he pulls up at the leisure centre, he puts the handbrake on and turns and studies me for a moment, his arm across the back of my seat. 'See, Eva,' he says, his eyes fond. 'We can still joke about it all. Nothing's ever that bad.'

And even though I know, and he knows, that some things are just so awful they can't be put right by having a laugh, he's made me feel a whole lot better, so I grin back at him and say, 'See you later, Farty-Pants!' and hop out quickly, giggling as he pretends to shake his fist at me through the windscreen. I'm still giggling as I enter the gym but then I see there's a meeting going on and I'm late so I slip into place hurriedly amongst the gymnasts sitting cross-legged at Mike's feet, between Rommy and Hannah who shuffle up to make room for me.

'Sorry I'm late,' I say, because I can see I've interrupted Mike in full flow, but he smiles down at me.

'That's OK, Eva. I was just extolling your virtues to everyone. You did a good job on Saturday.' I try to look modest, but inside I'm glowing. This is praise indeed from Mike. He goes on, 'You all did, in fact, minus the odd blip or two.' I can sense Rommy bowing her head in shame beside me; he doesn't need to say any more. 'Now it's time for you to move on, learn some new skills ready for the next competition.'

I nod eagerly, sitting up straight. Mum'll be pleased. Does he mean me personally, or everyone? It's brilliant starting on a new move, you get loads of personal attention from Mike. The next second he answers my question for me.

'Now we've got some new talent in the club, we can really go for it this year. You're going to be a cracking team, you seniors. I'm going to stretch each and every one of you and the first thing I'm going to do is bring our newcomer up to par with the rest of you. Then, when she's ready to take her place in the team with you four, and with new moves under your belts, we'll take the rest of the county by storm.'

'Hurray!' squeals Sophie, clapping her hands like a demented seal. She sets everyone else off shrieking and applauding. Everyone but me. Because I don't get it.

'What newcomer?'

It's a wonder he hears my question above the noise. But he does because he gestures towards the space the other side of Rommy. Only space is the wrong word, because that implies an empty area waiting to be filled but when I crane my head to peer past Rommy, I see this area is already fully occupied. In fact, it's packed solid, chock-a-block, full-house, standing-room only.

No need for me to tell you who's squatting in it like a ginormous, repulsive toad.

It's the brimming-all-over, grinning-all-over, Patty Slimey Williams.

'I swear she's stalking us!' I mutter furiously to Rommy and co. as we wait our turn for the vault. So much for new moves. We haven't had a look-in on the floor. Mike is too busy putting the toad through her paces, seeing what she's capable of.

It's quite a lot, as it happens. She leaps and pirouettes across the mats with an agility that is far from natural for a loathsome creature that should be crawling round on the bottom of a muddy pond. 'Elephant!' I spit, deciding to switch to a more appropriate animal image, when at last she comes a cropper as a fairly difficult somi ends in an awkward landing.

'I don't know, she's quite light on her feet,' says Hannah thoughtfully.

'For her size,' adds Sophie, placing her hands on her own slim hips.

'For an elephant,' I repeat, watching as Mike explains

to Patty what he wants her to do next. She tugs her leotard down round her bottom then pulls the neck up as she listens, as if she's self-conscious about her bum and her boobs. So she should be, and her belly and her bingo-wings and her thunder-thighs too. Then she places her hands on the floor and goes up into a handstand, supported by Mike.

'That was quite graceful,' says Rommy, by my side. Her quiet, non-judgemental tone infuriates me. Why does she always have to stand up for Patty? I can feel myself being consumed by vitriolic jealousy.

'Careful, Mike, I'd stand back if I were you. You don't want to be crushed when the twin towers fall.'

It comes out louder than I intended. Gravity makes my allusion obvious to everyone as Patty's boobs make a bid for ground zero, held in place only by an over-worked bra and the thin membrane of her leotard. A peal of laughter rings out as Sophie and Hannah get the joke and Patty, startled, loses her concentration and collapses heavily on the floor. Mike turns towards us. He looks angry.

Flip. I didn't mean him to hear it.

Nor her.

Her face is bright red.

Well, it's probably because she's been upside down. All the blood would have rushed to her head.

Rommy's looking at me in that way again. Like I'm something horrible that's crawled from under a stone. Like *I'm* a toad.

'What?'

She turns away from me and runs up to the vault, slamming her feet down hard on the board and launching herself over it at full pelt. She doesn't need to tell me what she's thinking, I can tell from the power and the fury of that vault.

Who does she think she is?

I'm *glad* Patty overheard me.

Fat slob.

The next day, Dad organizes time off work to take Mum to the doctor's. She comes downstairs looking pale and washed out and sits at the kitchen table, nursing a mug of tea. Her eyes are cast down and there are dark circles beneath them. I want to catch Rommy before school and time's going on so I don't bother with breakfast but she doesn't even notice. Not a good sign. When I say goodbye to her, she answers, but she doesn't look up.

Please let her be here when I get home.

I run round to Rommy's flat. She won't be expecting me, but hopefully I'll catch her before she leaves. I need my best mate this morning. When Mum gets like this throws me, it's like the time my security blanket disappeared, my Piece of Cold, I feel scared and alone. I need everything else to be normal around me. Rommy's good at making me feel better about myself, even though she has absolutely no idea about Mum's black periods. But she always seems to recognize when she needs to be there for me.

But not this morning. When I get to her front door, her mum is just on her way out with Rommy's kid brother and sister. She looks surprised when she sees me.

'Hello, Eva, love. You've missed Romilly, I'm afraid. She left early. I thought she was going to meet you.'

'Was she?' I look at her blankly. I couldn't recall last night arranging to meet up with Rommy. In fact, if I remember rightly, we didn't really talk much after that little joke of mine backfired, we just got on with practising our vaults. Candice, Rommy's little sister, peers up at me, bright as a button, a knowing look on her pointy little features that would be more at home on someone forty years older.

'She said she was going to meet a friend,' she points out. 'She didn't say she was going to meet Eva.'

Her mum tuts. 'She doesn't miss a trick, this one. And who else would she be meeting if it wasn't Eva, Little Miss Know-all?'

Who else indeed? 'I must have forgotten . . .' I mutter and turn away.

When I get to school, Rommy is sitting with Patrice on the front steps (what a surprise!) deep in conversation with Hannah and Sophie. Sophie spots me and waves and the others turn round. Rommy's face lights up; Patty's darkens. She shuffles up and makes room for me next to Rommy.

'Where've you been?' asks Rommy. 'I was afraid you weren't coming!' My heart lifts. The bell rings and we get up to file in through the door. Patty goes to follow Rommy and I glare at her. Automatically, she drops back and I link my arm through my best mate's and we walk into school together as we always do.

'Why were you late this morning?' asks Rommy, when we're in registration. Mr Simons is fussing over Patty at the front of the class, sorting out her timetable. I'm in a bad mood again. I've just discovered that she's in practically all of my lessons. What's even worse is she's in *absolutely* all of Rommy's.

'I went to call for you. Your mum told me you'd gone to meet a friend.'

Rommy looks stricken. 'Eva, I'm really sorry.'

I shrug my shoulders as if I'm too hurt for words. I know Rommy of old, she's really kind-hearted. She can't bear to think she's upset anyone. Especially me, her best friend.

It works. She blurts out, 'I went to meet Patty. She

asked me last night at gym club. She was really nervous about walking into school on her own today.'

'*Why?*'

'I suppose it's hard starting a new school in Year 9. She doesn't know anyone . . .'

'She knows you. She knows Hannah and Sophie. She knows *me* . . .'

Rommy shifts uncomfortably. 'Well, that's just it, Eva. She's a bit scared of you.'

'Me! Why is she scared of me?' I stare at Rommy round-eyed with injured innocence. She blunders on, not wanting to hurt my feelings.

'She overheard what you called her.'

'What?' I wrinkle up my face as if I'm trying to remember. 'What did I call her?'

'Fatty Patty.'

'She wasn't meant to hear that!'

'I know! But you called her the twin towers too . . .'

(And a fat slob and a gigantoraptor and a toad and an elephant and a blob and a . . . you don't know the half of it, Rommy.) 'That was a joke!'

'That's what I said! I told her you didn't mean it! But she's very sensitive about her weight.'

Can lumps of lard be sensitive? I glance at Rommy, her kind, pretty face full of concern, and I think to myself, you're such a nice person, Rommy, I don't deserve you.

Because if you knew what I was really like you wouldn't want to be my best friend. You wouldn't want to know me at all.

And for one awful moment I think I'm going to break down, like Mum, and bawl my head off in front of everyone, because I can't bear it any longer.

But luckily for me, I'm saved by the bell and instead I go off to my first lesson, arm in arm with my best mate, clutching her tightly, because I'm all at sea and she's my lifebelt, and if I don't cling on tight to her, I might drown.

When I get home from school, I can hear someone banging about in the kitchen.

'Mum?'

Dad emerges, wiping his hands on a tea towel. My face must have fallen because he says, 'It's OK, love, she's in the garden with the boys.'

I can feel my body flooding warm with relief. I cover it up, trying to sound casual.

'Same as usual then? More pills?'

He hesitates. 'No, not this time. There's a new doctor at the surgery. He's got a different approach. I'll let her tell you.' I must have looked alarmed because he adds quickly, 'It's nothing to worry about.'

Really? Every time I've heard those words in the

past it's meant there's something going on.

'I'll go and say hello then.' I move towards the back door but Dad says, 'No. Go and get changed for gym first then come and have some lemonade in the garden. Go on, Eva, do as you're told.'

Something's up, I know it is. I pull a face at him but do as he says. It's become a habit now, over the past four years, doing what my parents expect of me.

Upstairs, I poke my head round Amber's door. She's standing by the window looking down into the garden. I knew she'd be around, what with all that's been going on. She's got some sort of sixth sense, she always puts in an appearance when trouble's brewing.

I stand behind her and look over her shoulder. She's watching the others on the manicured lawn which is bordered by luxuriant flowering shrubs and brightly coloured annuals. It looks like an advert for *Homes and Gardens* with the boys sprawled on the grass and Mum, facing us, reclining on a lounger, her arm behind her head. She looks tired but relaxed. Dad comes out with a tray laden with glasses and a plate of cakes and a tall jug of iced lemonade, and places it on the wrought-iron table. The boys sit up and help themselves, their backs to me. Dad sits down next to them on one of the chairs and hands Mum a glass and she sips it gently through a straw then leans back again against the lounger, cradling the drink in her hands. You can hear their voices floating up, muted and disembodied, like a radio left on in another room.

'Summer days,' says Amber quietly and sighs. My heart goes out to her: she's almost unrecognizable as my confident, feisty sister in this pensive, nostalgic mood. I place my hand on her shoulder. There's nothing of her.

'I'm bigger than you are now,' I say, surprised.

She straightens up and looks at me, her eyes challenging, the old Amber again.

'You're not!' she says, indignant.

'I am!' It's so easy to fall back into our competitive roles.

'Back to back!' she orders and obediently I turn and stand with my back against hers, stretching up as far as I can. I can feel her shoulder blades, sharp against mine. Her hand moves over our heads and brushes my hair.

'You're on tiptoes!' she accuses, knowing me of old.

'I'm not!' I lie. I lose my balance (I swear she's given me a shove) and fall giggling on to her bed, curling up into a ball with my eyes closed, half expecting her to pummel or tickle me till I cry for mercy, but nothing happens. When I open them I see she's standing back at the window again, looking down at the garden, and she's waving. I jump off the bed and run to her side.

Down below, Mum is staring up at the window, wide-eyed. One hand moves up to her throat and the other one waves back, almost imperceptibly. Her glass tips over, draining her lemonade into her lap, then falls on to the lawn but it doesn't smash. This time it's me who gives Amber a shove out of the way. Dad and the boys turn around to see who Mum's waving at.

I stand there and wave at them all, feeling totally goofy. They all stare up at me and Dad frowns, then he turns back and pulls out his hanky and mops at Mum's skirt. He picks up Mum's glass from the ground, pours her more lemonade and passes it to her. Even from here, I can see that her hand is shaking.

'You gave me quite a turn,' says Mum, when I change into my gym kit and go outside to join them. 'For a moment I thought you were Amber. What were you doing in her room?'

I give her a hug. She feels insubstantial, like Amber, all skin and bone. Am I the only female round here with any flesh on them?

'Nothing. Just watching you all. Sorry, Mum, I didn't mean to startle you.' I sit down at her feet, my elbow on her knees, avoiding the wet patch where the lemonade has spilt on her skirt. I can feel her hand still trembling ever so slightly as it moves forward automatically to smooth back my hair. I glance up to see if Amber is still watching us but there's no sign of her. I give a big sigh and lean back against her.

'Can I have a chocolate éclair, Mum?'

'Go on then, just this once. Better have a banana as

well, give you some energy, then we can have supper when you get home from gym.'

Mum's in charge again. I reach for the biggest, most chocolatey cake I can find and sink my teeth into its creamy softness. Bliss! Then I remember and turn to face her, saying indistinctly, 'Mum! Dad says you've got something to tell us.'

'Yes.' She looks up again at Amber's window and then nods, as if it's helped her to reach a decision. I stop chewing, my mouth full of choux pastry and cream, suddenly aware that what she's about to say is very important indeed.

'I'm going to go for some counselling. I should have done it years ago.'

Is that all? I swallow my mouthful of sweet gooey stodge and take another bite, studying her. She's pale and exhausted-looking, as if she hasn't slept for weeks, but her mouth is set in a straight determined line as if she's really made her mind up about this. My eyes move to Dad who has a similar sort of expression on his face, as if it's a huge decision they've both made, together. I'm aware that both Ben and Zac are studying them intently as well.

'That's good . . . isn't it? We have counsellors at school we can talk to if there's anything wrong. Not that I've ever needed to see one,' I add hastily.

Mum's eyes close momentarily, as if she's in pain. Then she says, 'Yes, this new doctor at the practice thinks it would be good for me to talk to someone. I've kept everything bottled up for too long.'

No one says 'What about?' No one says a thing. I almost expect Dad to stand up and slap his thigh and say, 'Right then, sorted, now I'm off for a run.' Because we're like that in this family, we like things tidy, done and dusted, and put away.

And to be honest, I'm wondering what the big deal is. Bit of counselling – so what? Sophie went for weeks when her mum and dad split up, but I know, because she told me, it was just so she could get out of maths. I finish my éclair and lick chocolate off my fingers. Yummy. We don't get too many sticky treats in this house. I take a surreptitious peek at my watch and wonder if Mum's up to running me to gym tonight. I don't want to be late again.

But everyone keeps on sitting there.

Then Ben clears his throat and asks, 'So then, Mum, how often will you go for this counselling? Once a week?'

'And for how long?' I chip in, so she doesn't think I'm not interested, though now I've seen the time I'm starting to worry if Patty will get to gym early and Mike will start working with her again and the rest of us won't get a look-in. Or maybe she'll pair up with Rommy and . . .

'Well actually . . .' says Mum, casting a look at Dad as if she needs a bit of help. 'It's a residential course. I'm not sure for how long . . .'

'As long as it takes,' says Dad firmly. 'You take your time. There's no rush.'

'You're going away?' I stare at her blankly. 'Where?'

'Not far,' says Mum, looking anxious. 'But I have to stay there. It's the way the course is set up.'

Suddenly, my stomach decides to regurgitate my newly ingested chocolate éclair and ricochet it back up into my throat. I'm overwhelmed by a flood of memories from when Mum disappeared that time.

I cried myself to sleep for a month.

I refused to eat.

I wouldn't take a shower.

I got into trouble at school.

I did other stuff so bad I've blocked it out.

Till now.

Like, for instance, when Mum came home at last, I wouldn't speak to her, but then she put her arms round me and I went mad. I screamed the place down. I lashed out at her. I hit her and bit her and scratched her and kicked her. But she wouldn't let me go and, at last, I gave up and sobbed my heart out and let her cuddle me. Then she cried too and promised me she'd never, ever, leave me again.

She *promised* me!

But I was only a kid then.

'What about us?' I blurt out, before I can stop myself. At least I don't say, 'What about ME?' which is what I really mean.

'Alan, maybe this isn't such a good idea after all,' says Mum, a hint of desperation in her voice.

'Nonsense,' says Dad heartily. 'We can manage without you for a while, for goodness' sake. It's not as if any of you lot are little kids any more.'

'We'll be fine, Mum,' says Ben, frowning at me. 'We can look after ourselves.'

'Yeah, we don't need you fussing round us any more. We're all grown up now, haven't you noticed?' chips in Zac. Mum smiles at him gratefully and he helps himself to another cake.

'Eva?'

I'm not, I want to say, I'm not grown up. Not inside, anyway. I need you around still. Things go wrong if you don't keep an eye on me. You *know* they do.

Don't leave me, Mum. Please.

I can change this. I've only got to say, 'I don't want you to go,' and she won't, I know she won't.

They're all watching me anxiously. They won't blame

me. Not now they're all remembering what I was like last time. They feel sorry for me.

I HATE people feeling sorry for me.

I shrug.

'Whatever. Can someone take me to gym?'

When I get there, something's going on. Everyone's sitting silently in a tight circle, staring at Rommy, then suddenly someone yells, 'You licked your lips!' and there's a mass groan and the circle breaks up, shrieking with laughter. I push myself through.

'What are you doing?'

Rommy gives me a big, jammy smile. Her cheeks are bulging so much she looks like a hamster and her mouth is so full she can't speak.

'Rommy was trying to eat a doughnut without licking her lips,' explains Sophie. 'It's impossible.'

'It's Patty's idea,' says Rommy indistinctly. She's got sugar all round her mouth. 'Have a go!'

'No thanks.' I look around at all the beaming faces. They're having a ball, without me. Patty's grinning so much she looks as if her face has split in two. I want to wipe that smirk off her face. 'I don't eat rubbish like that.' An image of a chocolate éclair floats before me but mentally I elbow it quickly out of the way.

Patty's face falls, resuming its customary potato

shape. I glance over at the office where our coach is on the phone. 'Watch out Mike doesn't catch you. He'll go ballistic.'

Everyone looks uneasy. As if on cue, Mike finishes his phone call and he and Donna come out of the office. 'What are you lot up to?' he calls over. 'Why aren't you warming up? I've been watching you.'

Everyone springs up and Patty grabs the bag of doughnuts. Too late. 'What's that?' asks Mike curiously.

Patty looks terrified. 'We were seeing if anyone could eat a doughnut without licking their lips. Sorry. It was my idea.'

Wait for it! Recently, Mike and Donna, the other coach, have been giving us leaflets to read about nutrition. They're well into healthy eating, always prattling on about good versus bad carbs. Donna frowns. Oh dear, the honeymoon is over and Precious Patty is about to feel the full force of our coaches' wrath and discover that gym is a serious business after all. What a shame!

'I'm good at that game!' Mike's face lights up with delight. 'Give us a go!'

'What? Mike, you can't be serious!' Donna says, but she's laughing.

Mike picks up the bag and offers it to her. 'Come on, make it a contest! First one to lick their lips is a loser!'

Donna shakes her head at him as if he's taken leave of

his senses (which he has), then suddenly she laughs and says, 'Easy!' and takes a doughnut.

Everyone giggles and gathers round. Mike and Donna stand opposite each other and Mike takes one from the bag and springs into a fencing pose, brandishing his doughnut.

'We fight to the death,' he announces and takes a bite. Donna chuckles and follows suit, chews, swallows and immediately licks her lips.

Mike brays in triumph. 'Loser!'

'Eat it all!' commands Patty. Who does she think she is? I watch in amazement as Mike obediently carries on biting, chewing and swallowing his doughnut, egged on by an admiring crowd of gymnasts, without once allowing his tongue to lick up any stray grains of sugar that might be left on his lips. As he swallows his last piece he throws his arms in the air and declares, 'Result!' and everyone leaps up and down and claps and cheers as if he's just won a perfect 10.

And Patty Doughnut Williams even thumps him on the back and shouts, 'Champion!'

Uggh! It's enough to make you sick!

'What sort of example are you setting these girls, Mike?' asks Donna, but I can tell she doesn't mean it; she's giggling her head off.

Mike pretends to be indignant. 'It's their fault, they're

a bad influence,' he says, wiping his mouth on the back of his hand. 'They're all as bad as each other.'

Rommy looks at me. 'Eva's not,' she points out. 'Eva wouldn't have one.'

Trust Rommy to stick up for me. I glance at Mike, waiting for him to praise me. And he does.

'Good for Eva,' he says, then claps his hands. 'Right, you lot, get started.'

Everyone finds a space and starts their warm-up at last. I go through the motions perfectly, my body fine-tuned, but my mind is all over the place. I should be feeling really smug now, being singled out like that for Mike's approval. But I'm not.

Because something about his tone meant it didn't feel like approval.

It felt like criticism.

Mum doesn't waste much time. The next morning when I come downstairs, her bag's already packed and waiting at the front door and the next minute the taxi's here and there's just time for a quick hug and a kiss and an anxious, 'You'll be fine, won't you, sweetheart?' in my ear, and she's gone, without waiting for an answer. I don't even get a chance to wave goodbye, because I'm still in my pyjamas, which are soooo comfy but very old and grey because they've been washed so many times, and I'm not going outside in those for everyone to see me.

'I didn't know she was going that soon,' I say to Dad, bemused by the speed of it all.

He picks up his briefcase and grabs his jacket from the coat-stand. 'Better this way, love,' he says. 'They had a place ready so what's the point in hanging about?'

So I can get used to the idea?

So I can have second thoughts about it?

So I can tell her it's not such a good idea after all, it doesn't work? Sophie still hates her dad for going off with that bitch from the tennis club.

So I can persuade her to change her mind?

I can think of a hundred and one reasons why my mum should not go off and abandon us all in such a rush like she's just booked a last-minute holiday on the Internet and has to fly like NOW!

It must have shown in my face because his eyes soften and he rubs me gently on the arm. (Very unusual this, Dad doesn't go in for touchy-feely, he's more likely to give me a punch if anything, if he's feeling happy.) 'She'll be back before you know it,' he says and his quiet kindness makes me well up inside. But he's turned away and is going out of the door so he doesn't see I'm close to tears. 'See you tonight, love,' he says over his shoulder. 'And get those two lazy lumps out of bed!' The door slams behind him.

Good old Eva, you can always rely on her. I swallow hard then go to the foot of the stairs and bellow, 'Ben! Zac! Get up! You'll be late!' Then I eat a handful of cereal from the box to keep me going and go for a shower in Mum's and Dad's room, because I can hear one of the boys has already beaten me to it in the bathroom.

Mum's clothes are strewn all over her bed as if she's been having a trying-on session before deciding what to pack. Like you do when you go on holiday. 'Something comfortable for the day, something pretty for the night,' she'd chant to Amber and me as we packed our cases for our *gîte* holidays in France every summer. I wonder if she's taken something pretty for the nights on this *residential* counselling course of hers? Somehow I manage to refrain from checking her wardrobe and blast myself with red-hot water from the shower instead.

By the time I'm dressed and have got my stuff together, Ben and Zac have left for school. Downstairs, the kitchen table is littered with the remains of their breakfast. I pile the cereal bowls, knives, spoons and mugs in the dishwasher, brush the toast crumbs into the bin, stick the milk back in the fridge and wipe over the butter, marmalade and milk-smeared table with a cloth. There, that will do. Then I remember that I haven't had my breakfast yet. I glance at the clock. It's too late now. I'm not hungry anyway, I'll have something at lunchtime.

At school, the others are still going on about Mike and Donna as if the pair of them were pistols at dawn or up to no good in the equipment cupboard or something mind-blowing instead of actually competing to eat a doughnut. Big deal! Patty's hanging round as usual. This is particularly annoying this morning because I want to tell Rommy that Mum's gone away. I'm not going to tell her why though, I'm just going to say she's gone on a short break, which she has in a way. But it's important that I tell her, just because then I can stop thinking about it all the time, though I don't want to tell her in front of everyone, so I bide my time.

But, unfortunately for me, Fatty Patty seems to have acquired celebrity status because of her AMAZING DOUGHNUT COMPETITION. Everyone wants to hear about it and then everyone wants to try it. At lunchtime, Rommy disappears to the canteen with Patty and comes back with a huge pile of doughnuts, then Sophie, never one to miss a trick, has the enterprising idea of selling them at an inflated price on the understanding you can double your money if you can eat one without licking your lips. Soon a crowd has collected round them and the Jimmies are raking in the money faster than you can say 'Dunkin' Do-Nuts' and everyone's having a ball. Except me.

Because I want to get Rommy on my own and tell her about Mum.

And I'm famished!

The thing is, I want to go for lunch, like we always do, the Jimmies, all together. I haven't had any breakfast, remember. But now the doughnut competition is going with a swing and nobody wants to stop. Zac has a go (only because it's an excuse to hang around

Rommy), then all his mates from Year 10 come over to see what's going on and before you know it, there's not just a massive crowd around us all, but a queue has formed of prospective competitors stretching halfway round the school.

'Coming for lunch, Rom?' I ask, but she shakes her head.

'How can I? Look at all this lot waiting for a go.'

'But I'm starving!'

'Here,' says Patty, thrusting a bag in front of me. 'Have a doughnut!'

I'm dying to take one but there's no way I would from her. I mean, just who does she think she is? Last week she didn't even belong to this school; this week she's running the show.

'No thanks, some of us have figures we care about.'

Someone in the crowd says, 'Oo-ooohh!' and everyone laughs. Patty's face flushes.

'Hannah! Sophie! Come on, let's go and get lunch.'

Hannah hesitates. 'We're a bit tied up here.'

I glare at her and turn on my heel and march off to the canteen. They must have changed their minds pretty quickly, because when I get to the counter, they appear at my elbow. There's hardly anything left and I am just about to treat myself to pie and chips but when they appear I take the tomato and mixed-leaf salad instead. So do the other two. We spend a miserable five minutes poking it round our plates in the deserted canteen. Outside, roars of laughter proclaim another kid falling victim to the sugar temptation.

'I don't see what Rommy sees in her,' I say, cutting my rocket viciously into tiny pieces. I've learnt my lesson the hard way with the killer salad.

'Who?' Hannah spears a final slice of tomato into her mouth and puts her fork down, looking glum.

I nod towards the school yard. 'Old Doughnut out there.'

Hannah looks puzzled. 'Doughnut?' Then she laughs. 'Patty, you mean?'

I shrug. 'Good a name as any. She's round, sweet and sickly, and full of carbohydrate.'

They both giggle, then Hannah sighs. 'I'm still hungry.'

'Get a cake,' says Sophie. 'I'm going to.'

'Can't. They're all out there, remember?' says Hannah gloomily.

'They're no good for you anyway,' I say grimly. 'You don't want to end up looking like Doughnut.'

'D'you think I'm putting on weight?' asks Hannah anxiously, pinching her tight, flat stomach into a minuscule roll of flesh.

'No.' I can hear Mum's voice. 'But you will do if you eat rubbish.'

'Like Doughnut,' says Sophie thoughtfully.

'Exactly,' I say with grim satisfaction. 'Exactly like Doughnut.'

I'm a bit light-headed by the time I get home from school. I get like this if I don't eat regularly and one miserable bunch of leaves is all I've had all day. I wonder what's for tea, then I realize that Mum's not around for me to ask. Suddenly it occurs to me how completely we rely on Mum in this family to provide us with our daily sustenance.

Fortunately, Dad comes home early. He drops his briefcase in the hall and makes for the stairs, loosening his tie.

'Going for a run?'

He nods. 'Good day?'

'Not bad,' I lie, then, 'What's for tea?'

He looks blank for a minute, then runs his fingers through his hair. 'Um – I'll pick up some fish and chips on my way back.'

I shake my head. 'I've got gym tonight, I'll have something when I get home. Can you take me?'

He makes that clicking noise on the roof of his mouth he does when he's annoyed, then he nods. 'Come on then, I'll drop you off now, then I can get in a run before I have to pick you up again.'

I didn't mean now! But it's too late, he's back out the front door before I can point this out. I'm interfering with his plans, you can tell; he makes it sound as if I'm being a pain. So I refrain from objecting and charge upstairs to grab my stuff. In the car I stare morosely through the windscreen and pray silently that Mum comes home soon to be at my beck and call again. Then when I get to the leisure centre I have to hang about for ages waiting for gym club to open up, with no one to talk to and nothing to eat and I'm starving. It's not fair. I can't even get myself a bar of chocolate from the machine because Dad's rushed me out of the house so quickly I've forgotten my purse.

When gym finally gets going it turns out to be one of those nights when I can't do a thing right. We're working on the vault, which I'm normally really good at, but tonight everything's an effort. It doesn't matter which one I try, handspring with full twist or a half-on, half-off, I just don't seem to have any energy. My legs are a dead weight hanging off my body.

In contrast, the rest of the Jimmies are flying over the vault, even Sophie who's normally not too keen on it either, and they're all really pleased with themselves.

That's bad enough, but it's Doughnut who really gets my goat.

When she starts off, her technique's awful, she's

like a juggernaut thundering up to the board. 'Stand well back,' I warn the others helpfully. 'You don't want to get flattened!'

She launches herself into the air, attempting a straddle. Her legs are all over the place and her foot gets caught on the corner of the horse and she crashes to the floor. Mike comes running over and Rommy dashes to her aid, but she's on her feet immediately, more embarrassed than anything, though she is holding her side.

'The floor copped it more than she did,' I mutter to Sophie but I follow her and Hannah over to see what damage has been done.

'You all right, Patty?' I ask considerately, generous now that I can see how rubbish she is.

'Yeah, just winded,' she says, bending over to catch her breath, but not before I see the look of surprise on her face. Eva being nice to her? Whatever next?

'What did you do?' asks Mike.

'Caught my foot,' she explains, standing back up and taking a deep breath. 'I'm all right now, honest.'

'Right then,' says Mike. 'Try it again. I'll watch you this time.'

The next minute, the Doughnut's taken over the vault and sod the rest of us, we're just thrown off and left to prat about with Donna while Mike gives her his individual attention. Every so often he calls one of us up to demonstrate something, but he never calls me and I'm furious because if I'm so rubbish, why doesn't he give *me* some lessons? In the end I turn my back on them all and practise my backward walkover on the beam.

At the end of the session, Mike gathers us all around for one last go on the vault. The others shoot over it in straddle as if they haven't got a care in the world. This time I'm absolutely determined not to make a fool of myself again so I sum up all my strength and courage and go for a fairly complicated handspring and manage, at last, to pull it off.

'Well done, Eva,' says Mike and I smile smugly and go and stand by Rommy. 'Now your turn, Patty.'

'Nice one,' whispers Rommy to me and pats me on the shoulder.

'Thanks.' Patty moves to the end of the mat, ready for a run-up. 'This should be good,' I add with a snigger.

'She's fast,' says Rommy admiringly as Patty launches herself at the springboard. Her feet hit the board together, which protests loudly under her weight and her hands reach out before her. Then her legs lift off and open wide into leap-frog (no, leap-toad) and she soars over the board and lands in a perfect stretch position, back straight, arms extended above her head.

'Wow!' Rommy beams from ear to ear and bursts into

applause and everyone else joins in. Everyone, except me.
'That's amazing, Patty!'

'Quick learner,' says Mike, exchanging a look of triumph with Donna.

'She still can't do a handspring,' I mutter to Sophie, who's staring at Patty in amazement.

'She will soon at this rate,' she answers. 'Blimey Eva, she's good.'

It's been a rubbish day. To complete it, Dad's late, so I end up waiting on my tod in the car park for him to pick me up. Everyone's gone. Well, not quite. One person's still hanging around, but she's inside with the coaches. I'm sure they're arranging extra sessions for her. It's not fair, I'm going to tell Mum when I get home. Why should Fat Patty Williams get all the attention? I pay my fees same as everyone else!

Then it hits me, like a smack in the face. Mum's not there. I need her! I need her *now* to sort out what's going on. She could have a word with Mike, remind him he's our coach as well, not just Doughnut's. He won't listen to me, but he'd listen to her!

Only she's not around. She's gone away.

I can't help it but a sob forms in my throat, then another one, then before I know it, I can feel the tears spilling down my cheeks. I brush them away furiously, but it's too late, I've been spotted. There's a woman in the driving seat of an old grey car with flakes of rust on the side and she's watching me. She must be waiting for someone, because I can hear the radio on and it's some boring talk programme like Mum listens to when *she's* waiting for me and it makes me cry more. She switches it off and gets out of the car. Oh no, she's coming towards me.

'Are you all right, love?' she asks. I say nothing, hoping she'll go away. She doesn't.

'What's the matter?'

'Nothing.'

'Is someone picking you up?' Her voice is concerned and gentle and her eyes are kind.

'My dad.' I sniff loudly. My nose is running and I haven't got a handkerchief.

'I'm sure he won't be long,' she says. 'He's probably got caught in the traffic. Here you are, wipe your eyes.' She pulls a tissue out of her pocket and I accept it gratefully and scrub my eyes. 'Have another one,' she says tactfully and I blow my nose hard.

'I'll wait with you till he comes,' she says and puts her hand in her pocket again. 'Would you like a toffee?' She pulls out a crumpled paper bag and offers it to me. I take one, feeling about six, but I'm so hungry if she'd offered me a wad of wet-wipes I'd have grabbed one and stuffed it down my throat. I can feel myself calming down as its sticky sweetness assaults my taste buds. 'Oh dear,' she says, suddenly, looking guilty. 'I expect your mother told you never to accept sweets from strangers and here I am offering them to you.'

'That's OK, I'm not a little kid, you know.' I smile at her to take the sting out of my words and she smiles back. She reminds me of someone.

'Oh well in that case, might as well have another one.' She offers me the bag again and pops one into her mouth too. 'I love these, don't you?' I nod, my mouth full, and we chew companionably together for a while.

She's so nice. She doesn't fuss or ask me questions or anything, she just stands there giving me company and sustenance, like a big, warm St Bernard dog to the rescue, and I feel so much better, just for her being there. At last I spot Dad's car pulling into the car park. 'Here he is!'

'Oh good,' she says and moves away. Phew, she's not going to make a song and dance about me being upset to Dad.

'Thanks,' I call after her and she gives me a wave as she gets back in her car.

'Who's that?' asks Dad.

'I don't know, we were just chatting while I waited for you.' She's a nice lady but I hope I never bump into her again. She must have thought I was a right wally for blubbing like that. Now I've calmed down I'm embarrassed. 'Where've you been?' I ask grumpily.

'I'm not a flaming taxi!' Dad's tone is sharp. 'It's not easy, Eva, without your mum!'

I sigh heavily. You don't have to tell me.

Back at home the house is in darkness. 'Where is everyone?'

Dad shrugs. 'Haven't seen Ben, and Zac's at football training. I might as well go and get him now. Coming?'

'No, I'm starving.'

'I left you some fish and chips. Heat them up in the microwave.'

Thanks, Dad, you old gourmet, you. Congealed, batter-smothered, deep-fried delicacies from our local chippie, reheated by electromagnetic waves. Yum. Wonder what Mum would have to say about that? I'm so hungry I'm past caring.

Only when I switch on the light in the kitchen, I find even this tasty titbit is unforthcoming. Someone's beaten me to it. There's a note from Ben on the table.

'Thanks for the fish and chips. Back later.'

I don't believe it! All I've had today is a bowl of spinach and rocket and two toffees! I open the fridge. It's stacked with food, healthy Mum food. I rummage around in it and find broccoli, asparagus spears and a couple of avocados; a trussed-up chicken and a bowl of raw mince; carrots, sprouting green fronds from their heads, a bag of mixed lettuce leaves (no way!), weird-looking mushrooms and some peppers; a bottle of olives (yuk!); some strong-smelling cheese with suspicious blue veins in it; a pot of gunge that stinks of garlic and some horrible grey jelly-like things that look like snails but might be prawns; some squashy tomatoes, some dried-up chillies and some disgusting biotic yoghurt-type drinks.

Absolutely nothing I can eat.

How does Mum transform this lot into nice tasty meals, that's what I want to know. And where are the giant bags of cheese and onion crisps? Where are the Pringles? Where are the family packs of Mars bars and Snickers? And where are the pizzas, the quiches and the ready-made meals to heat up in the microwave because I'm a starving-hungry, cooking-phobic, total domestic-disaster of a teenager and I NEED TO EAT RIGHT NOW!

I have hunger pangs so crippling I could drop dead with malnutrition at any moment and all I have to ward off incipient collapse is a mouldy crust of organic bread, some soya spread and a squashed tomato.

I make myself a tomato sandwich and sit at the kitchen table, bravely prepared to enjoy my meal in noble solitary splendour. But then I take a couple of bites and realize the bread's got a sour, manky taste and it really has gone off and I chuck the sandwich in the bin because it's vile. Yuk! It's probably toxic! I've lost my appetite now completely and I decide to give up on this whole horrible day so I make a cup of tea and take it upstairs to bed with me.

I can't sleep though. I feel empty inside, which is hardly surprising. But it's not just my stomach that feels as if it's got a big hole in it, my chest has too. I press my hand against my ribs but I can't feel my heart beating. Someone's removed it and left a big, cold, gaping ache instead. I have no heart. I'm heartless.

A car pulls up. It's Dad, bringing Zac home. I can hear them going into the kitchen and Dad exclaiming, then Zac laughing. They've read Ben's note and Zac thinks it's a hoot. Even Dad chuckles but then he comes to the foot of the stairs and calls up, 'Eva?' I don't reply. 'Must be asleep,' he says and goes back into the kitchen and slams the door. After a while Ben comes home and joins them and there's a raucous belly-laugh as he's told he's eaten my supper. Now I hear the snap of cans being opened. What are they doing, having a party? If Zac's drinking lager, Mum will have a blue fit.

For a moment my stomach churns with hunger again but I don't get up to join them. In a perverse way, I prefer to lie here, listening to the deep undercurrent of male voices punctuated by roars of laughter, excluded from their tight, masculine circle. Nobody wants me; nobody likes me. Poor Eva. Tears well up again and soak my pillow, adding to my general sense of discomfort, and I curl up into a tight, unhappy ball and, at last, I find myself falling, falling, falling, into a dark, frenetic sleep.

It was bound to happen. It's the usual dream, the one where I'm running, but I'm making no progress. My feet are sticking. I wish I knew where I was going. I wish I knew what I was running away from. I turn around to look behind me and I see Amber. That's never happened before!

I'm so shocked I jerk awake and lie there trembling, thinking about my sister. Even though I'm awake, I'm trapped in another nightmare. The one that always comes back to haunt me. THAT MORNING.

After Mum tells her off I can feel her scowling at me as I gaze studiously out of the window, but I continue to ignore her. I have a big smirk on my face. She's furious.

'We had pizza last night after you went to bed,' she says suddenly, spitefully.

'Mu–um!'

'Amber . . .' says Mum, 'I warned you!'

'Sorry, Mum,' says Amber innocently. 'I forgot!'

'Why did you have pizza?' I cry, enraged.

'Ben brought it in,' says Zac, turning round from the front seat. 'It was yummy.'

'That's not fair!' I wail.

Mum turns round to glare at Amber. 'Did you have to?'

Amber stares at her round-eyed and righteous. 'I didn't expect her to be *jealous*!'

Zac raises his eyebrows. 'Yeah, right!'

Amber grins and pokes her tongue out at him. Then she digs me in the ribs and mouths, 'Yummy, yummy,' and rubs her stomach. I stretch out a hand and scratch her on the leg and two red wheals immediately appear. She howls in protest.

'OW! Mum! Look what Eva's done!'

Mum says, 'For goodness' sake, you two, I'm trying to drive!'

'LOOK!' yells Amber. 'It's bleeding!'

A minuscule drop of blood appears on her leg. She pinches the skin around it and a trickle spills down on to her knee. Mum looks over her shoulder and spots it.

'EVA! That is *so* naughty!'

'Watch what you're doing!' warns Zac as the car swerves. Mum looks back at the road. The back of her head and neck are ramrod straight with anger.

'If I crash this car,' she says furiously, 'it'll be all your fault!'

★ ★ ★

I sit up with a jolt, my heart thudding against my ribs as if it's trying to break out. At least I know it's working again. I need the loo. I get out of bed and pad softly to the bathroom. The house is silent now, well, almost, I can hear Dad and Ben snoring in stereo from their respective rooms. I wonder if Mum's asleep, somewhere far away on her residential course, or whether she's lying awake thinking of us.

On my way back I go into Amber's room and curl up on her bed. After a while I feel her hand resting lightly on my hair.

'Can't sleep?' she asks softly.

I shake my head and her fingertips move down to trace my brow, her touch as light and cool as an evening breeze.

'Amber?' I whisper. 'Do you hate me?'

She leans towards me and puts her mouth to my ear. 'You're my little sister, silly.' Her voice is a cold sibilant sigh in the night air. 'How could I hate you?'

I don't believe her.

In the morning I hear Dad saying, 'Eva?' like he's puzzled. I spring up but it's too late, he appears at Amber's door and says, 'So this is where you are!' I rub my eyes, waiting for the cross-examination, but Dad just grins at me and rumples my hair and says, 'You look about six when you've just woken up.'

He glances round Amber's room, a searching look as if he's seeing it for the first time in ages. He takes it all in: her medals hanging from the mirror; her badges sewn on to a quilt and positioned on the wall by Mum; her posters, her programmes, her certificates, her awards; her hair-straighteners and her hairbrush, not a single hair caught up in its pristine bristles; her lip gloss, her body-spray, her eye-sparkle; her belts, scarves and jewellery all hanging together in a bundle of riotous colour from pegs above her bed. All of them shouting, AMBER'S, KEEP OUT!

And he says, 'Maybe it's time you moved into here.'

'What?' I'm flabbergasted, I can't believe I've heard right. Quickly he adds, 'We'll see what your mum says. Grab a shower in the en suite if you want to,' and disappears downstairs.

I turn the shower on full, relishing the powerful jets of hot water that scald my body, blasting away the clammy clinging tendrils of the night. Me, take over Amber's bedroom! Get real, Dad. How would Mum feel about that?

How would Amber?

Afterwards I wrap myself in a big fluffy towel and step on to Mum's scales. They're her pride and joy, one hundred per cent accurate to the nearest microgram, and they measure your body mass index, your body-fat, body-water, and muscle-to-fat percentage. Dad reckons the only thing they can't do is make a cup of tea.

I bet she's missing them.

I wonder if she's missing me?

I have a surprise. A pleasant one. I've dropped nearly a kilo. I switch to imperial to check and see I'm down a gratifying two pounds. I jiggle about a bit and step off and back on again but it doesn't alter. Yay! Suddenly it occurs to me I'm encased in a massive bath sheet and I let it fall on the floor and stand there in the nude. I've dropped another pound.

I am soooo pleased. This is seriously good news. To be honest, I do have to watch my weight a bit; actually, that's not quite true, Mum watches it for me. The problem is, you see, I love my food. The creamier and more chocolatey the better.

But now Mum's not around and I've *lost* weight! Already!

I suppose I've been a bit all over the place lately, missing meals here and there. And yesterday, of course, was a total disaster.

Well, if this is the result of not eating for a day or two, I'm not complaining. I can't wait to tell Rommy.

I get dressed quickly. The waistband of my school skirt feels loose. Brilliant. Downstairs I root around in the cupboard for some cereal. Hmm, they must have been eating it last night, a beer and cornflake party, nice, because there's only the bran one left that tastes like sawdust (not that I've ever eaten sawdust, but it's how I imagine it would taste) and an empty packet of cornflakes. Like, hello? Why would you put an empty box back in the cupboard? I dispose of it in the bin, go to shove a piece of bread in the toaster then remember it's mouldy. (The bread, I mean, not the toaster!)

Dad's gone. My eyes fall on the large pile of change he's left for us. He's more generous than Mum. Then the penny drops. No Mum to give me a lift to school. It's not just lunch money, it's bus fare too. I glance at the clock. I'd better get a move on. No time for breakfast after all, I've got to leg it. Actually, I'm surprised to discover that I'm not that hungry.

As I'm going out of the door, Ben appears at the top of the stairs in his pyjama bottoms, looking a bit worse for wear.

'What time is it?' he asks.

'Late.'

'Is Zac up?'

'How would I know? I've got to go.'

He scowls at me and yells, 'Zac!' and disappears into the loo.

I miss the bus anyway. Damn. The doors close just as I get there and though the driver sees me, he pulls out into the flow of traffic and leaves me standing there like a lemon. From the back window, some Year 8 kids grin and wave at me. Pillocks!

Rather than hanging around waiting for the next bus to turn up, I decide to make my own way to school. Luckily we have PE today and I've got my trainers in my bag. I slip them on, hoist my bag over my shoulders and break into a jog, dodging the people on the pavement with their heads down, making their way to work. The rush hour traffic is head to tail and as I weave in and out of the crowd and nip across roads between the cars, I'm gratified to see the bus with the leering kids up ahead, stuck at the traffic lights. Someone spots me, points me out and they all turn round to watch me. Immediately I up my pace and streak past, head in the air, arms pumping. Their faces fall.

By the next set of traffic lights, they've caught me up and passed me again, jeering and gesticulating rudely from the back. I don't care. Ahead I can see the bridge where vehicles are at a standstill. I am now totally determined to get to school before them.

Once again I dig in, my legs striding out, my feet pounding the pavement beneath me. In seconds I'm past them and they boo me, their hands cupped around their mouths, and point their thumbs downwards, but I don't lessen the pace. It feels good, running like this, my heart thudding solidly against my ribs, my hair streamed out behind me, my feet drumming a steady beat on the pavement.

I get overtaken twice more. The kids are in a frenzy now, jumping up and down on the back seat, bawling insults at me which I can't hear, though I can tell from the actions that accompany them they're incredibly rude. It's become a duel now, a fight to the death, between them and me. Even the driver seems to be part of it, because I could swear he's driving twice as fast as usual, the bus rocking from side to side as he hurtles by. When he has to let someone off at the stop before school, his face is grim as I streak past.

It's downhill all the way now. I risk a glance over my shoulder. Behind me, the bus has its indicator on and is trying to pull into the stream of traffic, but no one is letting it out. You're not supposed to do that, you're supposed to wait till the road is clear before you indicate, I remember Dad telling that to Ben when he was teaching him to drive. I laugh out loud, feeling a surge of pure joy. I'm going to do it, I am!

In front of me I can see a crowd of kids hanging round the school gates. I increase my pace till my lungs feel as if they're on fire and lengthen my stride, powering down the last fifty metres. Before me, people start to clutch each other's arms and point: behind me, I hear the whine of the bus and I turn round for a quick peek. It's pulled out at last and it's bombing down the road behind me. The crowd start cheering, they've sussed what's going on. The bus is going fast, but it will have to slow down soon. Unlike me.

The next minute I charge, full-pelt, into the crowd, knocking a few kids flying. Hands grasp at me, steadying me as I stumble, then someone thrusts my arm in the air. It's Rommy.

'She beat the bus!' she yells in awe. 'Eva beat the bus!'

I bend over, hands on my knees, gulping air into my

parched lungs, each breath like a raw wound in my chest. My legs are like jelly, my whole body's shaking like I've got St Vitus's dance, my head feels as if it's going to explode, but when a cheer goes up from the crowd, I think I could die from happiness.

Funny how days are like that. Some days start off rubbish and get worse as they go on, others start well and get better. This turns out to be a brilliant day (about time too!). It starts to rain so we can't get out to play netball (that's not good, don't get me wrong) but Mrs Ellis says we'll do some health and fitness instead and we all groan, because that's not good either. Health and fitness is a euphemism (lovely word, meaning a polite way of saying something) for the girls being crammed in the hall to watch an ancient video on some old crone from the eighties with big hair doing aerobics in a pink leotard while the boys play basketball in the gym.

But we must have run through the complete gamut of Portland High PE department's video shelf because today Mrs Ellis says to Mr Jones, rather sharply I thought, 'Your turn for the hall, I think,' and marches us off to the gym before he has time to object. When we get there, Sophie grabs a ball and starts lobbing it through the hoop but Miss says in her best do-as-you're-told voice, 'Put that back immediately, Sophie, and come and sit down!'

She tells us to divide up into eight teams and sit cross-legged, one behind the other. Of course, I make sure the Jimmies are all in one line and Doughnut's in another. It's not hard. 'You're in that team,' I point out helpfully as she tries to sidle in behind Rommy, and direct her to the one next to us. She looks a bit crest-fallen but moves over obediently.

'Now then,' says Mrs Ellis, setting out four cones immediately in front of us and another set at the opposite end of the gym, 'we're going to test your fitness.'

She gets a box out of the stock cupboard and hands everyone in our team a small cassette player.

'Are we dancing?' asks Sophie, jiggling about on her bum, all excited. 'What's your favourite music, Miss?' Honestly, she gets hyper at the tiniest change from routine. Mrs Ellis treats her to the full benefit of her glacial glare.

'*When* you're quiet, I'll explain,' she says severely. Sophie shrinks back into silence. 'Give these out to every second team please, Sophie.'

When we're all ready with half of us clutching the tape recorders, Mrs Ellis says, 'Right then, listen carefully. We're going to do some bleep tests. Anyone know what a bleep test is?'

My hand shoots up. 'Eva?'

'It's where you have to run between the cones in time to the bleeps.'

'That's right.' She smiles at me. 'I suspect you'll be very good at this. I heard about your race with the bus this morning.'

I smile back at her, feeling my face flushing. Wow! Even the teachers are talking about it. Then she adds, 'But you must be careful, Eva, you really shouldn't race buses you know, it's dangerous.'

'I wasn't, Miss,' I lie. 'I was just running to school.'

'Very commendable,' she nods approvingly. 'The rest of you should try it.'

She runs through the test explaining how we have to do twenty-metre shuttle runs. 'The test consists of twenty-three levels. The time between the recorded bleeps decreases as you go up through the levels. It will test your maximum fitness.'

'Why haven't we all got a tape recorder, Miss?' Sophie asks.

'Because you're working in pairs. Your partner is the girl in the team next to you.' She fixes Sophie with a no-nonsense stare. 'You're working with me.' Sophie's face falls.

So much for my machinations. Guess who's sitting opposite me in the next team?

Doughnut.

She looks as unhappy about it as I do. I wonder if it's worth trying to swap but decide against it. I seem to be in Mrs Ellis's good books at the moment, let's keep it that way.

'You go first,' she says and I hand her the cassette player.

'Ready?' asks Mrs Ellis and we're off. It's fun this. I reach the other cone easily and am nearly back to the start before the bleep goes. Not everyone is as good. It's a bit chaotic at first with people not sure whether they have to stop or turn or keep on running when the bleep goes, but after a while we soon get the hang of it and start progressing up through the levels.

Well some of us do anyway. It's obvious straight away that some people are a lot fitter than others, not surprisingly, because there are some girls in my year for whom putting on their face slap is all the exercise they get while others are in pretty good condition. I have to say, all the Jimmies do themselves proud. It stands to reason we'd be in good shape, we do gym practically every day of our lives. Even Sophie gives Miss a run for her money.

I'm the last one left in. Finally the bleep beats me. 'Well done, Eva,' says Miss. 'Now swap over.'

Patty hands me the tape recorder. This should be good. If I remember rightly, the diplodocus is not exactly famous for its speed.

But I've underestimated her (as usual). Silly me, after

all, I've seen her in the gym. She's actually quite fast, well more than quite, she's VERY fast; what she lacks in technique, she more than makes up for in pace. She might look and sound like a steam roller but this girl moves more like a high-speed train.

Lucky for me, there are lots of bleeps going off all over the place. Lucky for me, I'm not the only one who seems to find it a bit difficult to work out which is my partner's bleep. Lucky for me, Mrs Ellis doesn't notice what I'm up to.

Not so lucky though for Patty Williams, who goes out in the early stages. Shame.

Not like me.

'You're up there with David Beckham,' says Mrs Ellis at the end of the lesson, clapping me on the shoulder. 'Wish we were all as fit as you.'

'Well done, Eva,' says Rommy, giving me a hug. She's come third and is overjoyed.

'Well done you.' I hug her back.

'Yeah, you're dead fit,' says Sophie, looking a bit annoyed. She was second (but a long way behind me!) and is green with envy.

'You did good,' says Hannah and squeezes my arm. I'm not sure where she came, but she seems pleased with her performance.

'So did you!' I smile, magnanimous in victory, and put

my arm round her too. 'We all did.'

'It just goes to show everyone that exercise is the key to fitness,' Mrs Ellis lectures to the rest of the class. 'All those girls that do gymnastics did really well.'

Sophie brightens up and wraps herself around Rommy, Hannah and me, planting a kiss on each of our cheeks. 'Well done the Jimmies!' she crows.

I glance at Patty. She's sitting with her back against the wall, head down, staring at the floor. Her shoulders are hunched, her arms are on her knees and she looks more lumpy than ever. I can't resist it. 'How did you get on, Patty?' I ask innocently.

She looks up at me, her face curiously empty. She's a doughnut with all the jammy bit chewed up and spat out of its centre. Her eyes move to take in the four of us standing together, united in our fitness.

'Not very well,' she says. Her voice is flat.

'Ahh, poor Patty,' cries Rommy. 'Never mind.' Her concern is genuine. Mine isn't.

'Yeah, never mind, Patty,' I reiterate in my best supportive tone. 'You can only improve.'

She fixes me directly, eyeball to eyeball. 'I tried my hardest.' She's not daft. She knows what I've done.

Rommy squats down next to her and says encouragingly, 'You just need to practise, that's all.' She smiles at Patty and gives her a little squeeze. Patty's eyes soften and she smiles back. I feel a twist of jealousy, so sharp it's like a real pain.

'Look, I don't mean to be rude . . .'

'But?' Patty looks at me coldly.

I wait a minute, then crouch down beside them, sitting back on my heels. 'Well, the thing is,' I say confidentially, 'you'd be a lot fitter if, you know, if you were . . .' I tail off as if I'm embarrassed.

'Not so fat?' Her voice is strong, challenging, in contrast to mine which sounds hesitant and awkward. I'm a good actress. I had an expert tutor, I watched Amber for years. She'd be proud of me now. I look suitably upset and Rommy jumps to my defence.

'No, Eva didn't mean that, did you, Eva? You didn't mean Patty was fat?'

'No, of course not. I meant thinner, that's all. Just thinner, not fat.'

'Eva's only trying to help,' bleats Rommy.

Patty ignores her and addresses me. 'I'm a fast runner,' she says stubbornly.

''Course you are. You'd be even faster if you weren't, you know . . . carrying so much weight.'

Rommy gasps.

'What?' I feign surprise. 'Look, I'm not being nasty, I'm only saying what everyone else thinks.'

Rommy looks appalled. 'Oh flip,' I gulp and look

round wildly. 'I'm useless at this, I didn't mean to be rude, Patty. I'd better shut up.'

I stand up suddenly and turn away as if I wished the earth would swallow me up, avoiding Sophie's eye. She's trying desperately not to giggle and I can't look at her or I'll break up laughing, especially when I catch sight of Hannah, who's looking totally bemused. I bite my lip and turn back to face them all, arms spread wide in appeal.

'I was only trying to help and now you all hate me. Me and my big mouth . . .' I break off, adding a little sob for good measure, and make for the door. I haven't gone very far when I hear Rommy calling, 'Eva! Eva, come back!' I grin to myself and rush out of the gym, the door swinging shut behind me.

Yes, on the whole, it's been a very satisfactory day indeed.

I start running to school regularly after that. The thing is, you wait ages for a bus and then when it comes it's full and you can't get on and you have to wait for the next one and then you're late. It doesn't seem to bother Zac for whom late detention is fast becoming a way of life, but it really bugs me. I mean, I've never been late in my life before, Mum's made sure of that, and now I'm getting it in the neck from my form teacher on a daily basis. One morning he has a hissy fit.

'This is your last warning, Eva. You'll have an hour's detention if you're late again tomorrow.'

'It's not my fault! I was there on time but the stupid bus went straight past me!'

But my equally stupid teacher isn't listening. He takes it as a personal affront if anyone comes in after the bell and has moved on now to gripe at the next unfortunate latecomer, Sophie, who actually does have a pathological problem in getting out of bed in the morning. We have a grumble about it at lunchtime.

'The thing is, I'm an owl, not a lark,' moans Sophie. 'It's a biological fact, I was born that way. I've tried to explain it to Mr Simons but he won't listen.'

'He never does,' I complain. 'So much for pastoral care. I thought teachers were meant to look after you. They're supposed to be *in loco parentis*.'

'What's that mean?'

'Standing in for your parents,' says a quiet voice. Patty Williams is loitering with intent as usual. I shoot her a look of venom. Know-all. Who does she think she is? *I'm* the clever-dick round here.

'Where *is* your mum by the way?' asks Rommy suddenly. 'I haven't seen her for ages.'

'Yeah, how come you're getting the bus anyway? She normally brings you, doesn't she?' chips in Sophie.

'We haven't seen her at gym either,' says Hannah.

Three pairs of eyes are staring intently at me. No, four; I can feel Doughnut's boring into me as well, nosy devil. 'What are you looking at?' I snarl. 'You don't even know my mum.' She drops her gaze but the other three continue to gawp at me. To my horror I feel my face getting warm and to cover up I snap, 'What is this, the Spanish inquisition? She's busy, that's all.'

'OK,' says Sophie, taken aback. 'Keep your hair on, we were only asking.'

'Well don't.' I turn on my heel before they *only* ask me why I've turned scarlet but as I march off I hear Sophie gasping, 'Moody or what!'

That afternoon I brood on what they've said. Trust them to notice Mum's not around. They've obviously been discussing it. I wonder what's going through their minds? I bet they think Mum's walked out on us all. Well, let them. I'd rather them think that than know the truth.

I decide it's best not to hang about waiting for a bus after school, they'll only start interrogating me again, gossipy gits, so I run home as fast as I can. By the time I get there, my lungs are on fire, my legs are aching and the sweat's pouring off me, and guess what? There's nobody at home and the house is a mess. What a surprise.

I set to, sweeping cans, crisp packets and the festering remains of half-eaten sandwiches into the bin and unload the dishwasher, filling it back up again with the toxic mountain of used plates, bowls, mugs and saucepans that is blocking the view out of the kitchen window, all the time cursing myself for having the misfortune to live with such a pack of idle, feral pig-swill, who I never actually get to see, I just clear up after. Mum, come back please, all is forgiven, I never realized you had so much to put up with! No wonder you need therapy!

And no wonder you're quite happy to stay away from home too, as long as it takes.

After that, I've hardly got the energy to rustle up something to eat, let alone worry any more what the others are saying about me. Rommy texts me a couple of times, but I ignore her. Instead, I make myself a Marmite sandwich (being as that's the only spreadable thing I can find in the cupboard) and sit down to watch telly.

After a while Dad comes home. 'Anyone in?' he calls from the hall.

'Just me,' I shout back. He goes into the kitchen and I hear him opening the fridge. Good, he'll notice I've cleared up. The next minute he appears at the door and I look up at him expectantly, waiting to be thanked. Then I notice he's got a can of lager in his hand.

'Aren't you going for a run?'

'Too knackered.' He takes a swig of his lager. 'Got gym tonight?'

'Nope, it's the juniors.'

'Good. Think I might go out for a drink then. You've eaten, have you?' He glances at my plate.

'Um, sort of . . .' But he's not listening.

'Right, I might as well have a bite to eat out then. Ben

and Zac can look after themselves, there's plenty in the fridge.' He loosens his tie.

'Tell them to clear up after themselves then,' I say sulkily. He hasn't even noticed.

'What?'

'I've spent ages tonight tidying up after them.' (And you, I add mentally, but wisely refrain from saying that out loud.)

He snorts. 'You're sounding more and more like your mother every day. Lighten up, Eva.'

I'm feeling more and more like my mother every day! I'll give him lighten up! Is that all the thanks I get after all my efforts? I'm so mad, I'm afraid I'll explode. Instead I stand up, give him a stinking look and flounce upstairs, taking a well-aimed kick at his briefcase standing innocently in the hall as I pass.

I slam my door shut and throw myself on my bed. After a while I hear Dad's feet on the stairs and then he knocks quietly and says, 'Eva?' but I ignore him. I hear the door opening and I can feel him studying me, even though I keep my eyes tight shut. After a while he clears his throat and says, 'Look, I know you're missing Mum . . .' and his voice is so gentle I think I'm going to cry so I sigh loudly as if I'm bored rigid and turn away from him to face the wall. He tuts with frustration and mutters something like, 'Oh, suit

119

yourself!' and shuts the door sharply and goes back downstairs.

I continue lying there with my face pressed up against the wall, as the tears squeeze their way through my eyelids to run, unfettered, down on to my pillow. I'm trapped in my well of self-pity and I can't climb out of it, not when Dad shouts up that he's off out, not when Zac comes in ages after, not even when I hear Ben staggering up to his loft bedroom hours later. (And if you think he gets that tanked up doing rugby training, Dad, then you must be dafter than you look. Oh, but you wouldn't know, would you, because you're out getting bladdered too?) And in the end I fall asleep.

The next morning, I get up before anyone else so I can catch an earlier bus, because I know Simple Simons will keep to his word and bang me in detention if I'm late again. But then, I don't plan it, it just happens, all of a sudden I break into a run, and go straight past the bus stop and on up the main road. Soon my chest is heaving and my mouth is dry but it's quieter at this hour of the morning, less traffic and people about, and I slow down, stretch my legs out and start to enjoy it. After a while my breathing settles down and it doesn't seem so hard any more, and before I know it I'm at school and my legs aren't aching half as much as they were the time before and I feel better. I've climbed out of the well.

So that's how I start running to and from school every day. All gain, worth the pain: Mr Simons has nothing to have a go at me about any more, I get to pocket the money Dad leaves me for my bus fare, and I feel loads better in myself. It's like all the magazines say, exercise is good for you, and one of the best things it does is it releases all these endorphins and makes me feel . . . happy, I suppose. Well, happy-ish.

AND . . . the biggest AND of all . . . I'm toning up beautifully with all this exercise.

'Look at you,' says Rommy admiringly one night at gym when I come off the balance beam. 'You're in great shape.'

'Yes,' says Hannah admiringly, 'you've got muscles in all the right places.'

'Have you lost weight?' asks Sophie suspiciously.

'I don't know,' I lie. 'Have I?'

'Looks like to me,' says Sophie. 'You've been on a diet.'

'No I haven't!'

This time I'm telling the truth. I'm not on a diet as such. I'm just not eating very much.

It's not intentional, it's just happened by accident. It started that horrible day when Mum went away and Doughnut had her eponymous doughnut competition, and I bet she doesn't know what that word means! (*Eponymous: one who has given his or her name to something, as in* Oliver Twist*, the eponymous hero.* We learnt it in English last year.) I had practically nothing to eat that day, nor the next, if I remember rightly. Then, when I started running to school every day, I didn't want to eat breakfast before I left because it made me feel sick and by the time I got there I didn't feel like eating any more.

At lunchtime I always choose salad now and I suppose I've got Doughnut to thank for that because I make a big show of healthy eating, just to make a point to Rommy that her new fat friend may be happy to stuff herself with starchy junk food but her old *best* friend isn't. Actually, this seems to have backfired a bit, because all the Jimmies do as I do and Doughnut follows suit, just as if she considers herself to be one of us, blooming cheek!

Then at suppertime . . . well, since Mum's not around, there doesn't actually seem to be a suppertime any more. Zac and Ben tend to fill up on pizza and oven chips from the freezer when they're around because now Dad's doing the shopping, it's crammed full of such goodies. When Dad comes in he says, 'Have you eaten, Eva?' and more often than not I've made myself a sandwich by then and I'm off to gym so I say, 'Yes' even though I know Mum would throw a blue fit if she knew because it's not what she would call 'eating'.

By the time I get home I'm usually totally zonked out what with all the running and gym and everything and the kitchen is looking like a war-zone anyway, so I just fall into bed and crash out for the first time in my life, even though my sleep is still disturbed by those weird dreams.

So, to be honest, I am aware that I'm not eating properly and I also know that I'm losing weight, because Mum's super-duper scales tell me so on a daily basis. But I'm *definitely* not following some stupid diet for saddos, like some people should be whose name I won't mention but that happens to start with PW (or D, for Doughnut, as she's affectionately known, ha,ha).

'It's all that running you're doing,' remarks Sophie. She makes it sound like I've taken up body-snatching or happy-slapping as a hobby. I can feel myself tingling with suppressed anger.

'Maybe you should try it,' I say sweetly. Sophie looks annoyed.

'Well, maybe I should,' she says, 'but personally, *I* wouldn't want to be hot and sweaty all day.'

I frown at her. '*I* don't smell!'

She raises her eyebrows at me and gives me a superior smile. 'I never said you did.'

'It's not sweat that makes you smelly, it's the bacteria beneath it,' I say icily.

'Is that a fact?' asks Rommy with interest.

'Don't know. Ask Smellody Melody!' shrieks Sophie

and makes a performance of sniffing her dainty armpit, which she has deodorized to odourless perfection this morning, and screwing up her fastidious little nose. Everyone laughs except Rommy, who casts an anxious glance around in case Melody's in earshot (she isn't), and me. I'm just dying to wipe the smirk off Sophie's face.

'So you reckon the only thing that's stopping you from running to school is you don't want to be smelly all day?' I challenge her.

'Definitely,' she says.

'Me too,' admits Rommy.

'And me,' chips in Hannah quickly.

I spot Patty hovering behind Rommy, hanging on to her every word as usual.

'What about you, Doughnut?'

Rommy gasps. 'Don't call her that, Eva.'

'It's because she introduced us to that brilliant game,' I say innocently. 'You don't mind, do you, Doughnut?'

Patty shrugs but her eyes are flinty. 'I could run to school,' she says frostily. 'No problem.'

I give a little snort. That would be a sight to behold. I don't believe any of them, anyway, not even Rommy.

So the next day I wait till we're all together waiting for school to open and Mrs Ellis's car pulls into the car park, then I announce loudly, 'Oh good, now before I forget . . .' and march up to her. 'Excuse me, Miss,' I say politely and clearly, making sure my audience can hear me, 'I wonder if I could have a word?'

Well, Mrs Ellis is only too pleased we're taking her health and fitness lessons so seriously, isn't she? 'Of course you can all use the showers before school. Well done, Eva, for getting your friends to run too. Marvellous exercise! You're an inspiration,' she beams and thumps me on the back enthusiastically.

So that's how I face up to Sophie, call everyone else's bluff, inflict further humiliation (I hope) on Doughnut and earn brownie points with my sports teacher, all in one fell swoop. Not bad for a morning's work and the day has hardly started. It's my turn to smirk at Sophie now. It's hard not to when you see the look on her face.

Mum phones. She's spoken to Dad a number of times but I'm always at gym. At last I get to talk to her. She sounds fine, just like herself on a good day.

'You are eating properly, Eva, aren't you? You're not filling yourself up with crisps and chocolate?'

'No, Mum.' If she only knew! I change the subject quickly. 'When are you coming home?'

There's silence on the end of the line. I feel a little tug of fear. 'Mum?'

'Soon, Eva, soon. Only it's a really intensive course, this one, and I don't want to put a time limit on it.' It sounds like an excuse. I don't say anything.

'It's doing me a lot of good, darling, I should have done it years ago.'

'What's it about?'

'Oh, this and that. You know, coming to terms with things, letting things go . . .' Mum's voice trails off vaguely.

'Dad's letting things go here . . .'

There's silence, then she says, 'I'm sure he's trying his best. You all need to pull together.'

I snort derisively then add, 'Can I come and see you?'

'No!' She's adamant. 'No, that's not possible. Dr Beerbaum doesn't want me to have visitors. He thinks it's best if I take some time out for a while.'

'Who?'

'Dr Beerbaum. He's my therapist.'

The tiny tug of fear twists itself into a hard knot in my stomach. I didn't know Mum was seeing some sort of shrink. Dr Beerbaum! What sort of weird name is that? He sounds like something out of a horror film.

Suddenly, an awful thought occurs to me. Perhaps she can't come home, perhaps she's been . . . what do they call it on television? Sectioned! Perhaps she's banged up in some horrible grim hospital with bars on the windows, held there against her will by the sinister Dr Beerbaum who plans to use her for his evil experiments.

'I *miss* you.' I sound like a six-year-old.

There's a silence. Then Mum says quietly, 'I know.'

'Come home, Mum,' I wheedle, sensing victory.

Her voice trembles. 'I'm sorry, Eva, but I need to be on my own to do this properly.'

'Do *what* properly? Lie on a couch and talk to your *therapist*?'

She takes a deep breath. 'It won't be for ever. I promise you.'

She's not going to give in. 'It's not fair! Mum, the house is a mess, Ben and Zac won't do a thing, I have to do everything and Dad doesn't care . . .'

'Don't be silly, Eva. I'll be home as soon as I can.' Her voice is level again now, crisper. It stops me panicking but it makes me mad.

'Fine.'

'Good girl. Now tell me what's been happening? How's gym?'

'All right.'

'What have you and Rommy been up to?'

'Nothing much.'

'How's your dad?'

'OK.'

She sighs. 'All right, sweetheart, I'll call you again soon.'

'Right.'

'Love you, Eva.'

She puts the phone down.

'Love you too,' I whisper, but it's too late.

She doesn't. She doesn't love me. If she did she'd be here at home, being a mum. She'd be looking after me, taking me to gym, cooking nice meals for me, keeping the house clean, doing my washing. I had to go to school today in the shirt I wore yesterday because Dad had forgotten to do a wash. Nobody else has to go to school in a grubby shirt, nobody else has to sort out their own washing . . .

I run upstairs and throw myself on my bed, tears of self-pity coursing down my cheeks. Downstairs in the hall the phone rings again and Zac answers it. 'Eva?' he calls but I yell, 'Go away!' From Amber's room I hear a chuckle. I get up and slam my bedroom door shut, then go back to bed to bury my face in the pillow.

If it was Amber asking her she'd come home, wouldn't she? She'd do anything for Amber.

After Mum shouted at us THAT MORNING in the car, Amber and I quietened down and looked out of our separate windows. It had started to rain and I watched the people on the pavements scuttling past on their way to work, like beetles scurrying this way and that, as I sat snug and dry in the back of the car, my lunchbox on my knee. Some, hunchbacked under umbrellas, looked like walking toadstools, their legs visible, like stalks, beneath the canopy and I remarked on it to Amber, but she ignored me. The traffic was heavy and Mum kept clicking her tongue and stopping and starting all the time, edging forward when she could. The windscreen wipers squished to and fro, like the hands of a manic clock, marking down the seconds.

'I'm going to be late,' fretted Amber. 'I'll get a detention!'

'And whose fault is that?' muttered Mum, jabbing her foot on the brake as the car in front of her came to an abrupt halt.

'Eva's.'

'No it isn't!' Amber's accusing voice jolted me from my reverie and I leapt automatically to my own defence. But it *was* my fault, probably. We were running late because I wouldn't eat my breakfast and Mum was tired.

I decided to investigate what was in my lunchbox. My fingers pressed the little button and the pink, plastic lunchbox swung open to reveal its secrets.

Two mysterious items confronted me alongside my cheese sandwiches, my drink and my apple. I opened the little silver foil package first, as thrilled as if I was unwrapping a birthday present, my excitement evaporating rapidly as a bundle of carrot sticks was revealed. Undeterred, I turned my attention to the other container, a small plastic box, tugging at the corner, gently at first, then harder, as the top refused to yield.

'Mum! Eva's eating her lunch!'

'Put it away, Eva,' said Mum automatically.

'I just want to *see*,' I protested and continued to pull with all my strength. Suddenly the top shot off and disgusting green gloop flew everywhere. It was in my face, my hair, my clothes, the back of the seats in front of me. I could even see some on Mum's hair.

'MUM!!!!!' Amber howled in anger next to me. Her school uniform was splattered with lumpy green globules and she'd got some on her face too.

Zac shrieked with laughter.

'What is it?' I asked bewildered. I stuck my finger in the mess. 'It looks like sick.'

'Guacamole,' said Mum bitterly. 'It's a dip. Avocados, onion, garlic and pepper with a touch of lime juice. Why do I bother?'

I licked my finger cautiously and shuddered. 'It tastes like sick too.'

'Mu-um!' screamed Amber as she tried unsuccessfully to scrape the gunk off her shirt. 'Do something!'

'What can I do?' snapped Mum. 'I'm driving!'

'Look at me!' bawled Amber.

Mum took a quick peek in her mirror and groaned, 'Eva!' She rummaged round in the pocket of the door and the car swerved alarmingly. 'Zac! There's a cloth in the glove compartment!'

Zac fished about and handed her an oily rag. 'Not me, silly! Give it to Amber,' she ordered.

Amber snatched her seat belt open, grabbed the rag off Zac and scrubbed furiously at her school uniform.

'It's making it worse! I've got oil on me now!' she wailed.

'Mum, Amber's got her seat belt off!'

'Shut up, Eva, it's your fault!' screeched my sister.

'Stop it, you two!' yelled Mum. 'Amber, put your seat belt back on.'

'It's everywhere! It's all over the seats as well! Mum, look!'

Mum turned her head and looked into the back. 'Eva!' she gasped. 'What have you done?'

That was the last thing I can remember her saying.

Zac puts his head around the door. 'You all right?' he asks.

'Yeah.' I rub my eyes with my sleeve and sit up. 'Got a bit of a headache. Who was that on the phone?'

'Romilly. She wants you to call her back.'

'What about? And it's Rommy, not Romilly.'

He shrugs. 'Girl stuff. Romilly's prettier.'

Prettier than whom? Me? Then I realize with relief he means the name, not the person. 'When are you going to ask her out, Zac?'

There's no reply. I look up and he's grinning at me sheepishly. My jaw drops.

'You have, haven't you? You've asked her out! What did she say?'

132

'She said "Yes".'

'Yay! At last!' I fling my arm up and punch the air. 'When did you ask her?'

'Just now. She wanted to speak to you and you were in a mood and she sounded so disappointed, someone had to cheer her up . . .'

'Aahh!' He looks all flushed and happy. The only time he's ever this pleased with himself is when he's coming off the football pitch. The phrase 'tickled pink' springs to mind and I put the words into action, leaping off the bed and grabbing him round the waist, my fingers plucking, prodding, squeezing, till he moans, 'Gerroff!' and seizes my wrists, dragging them off him, but he's laughing.

'When?' I ask, out of breath.

'When what?'

'Duh! When are you taking her out?'

'Saturday.'

'Where are you going?'

He shrugs. 'Cinema?'

'What are you going to see?'

'What is this, twenty questions? I dunno yet.'

'You'll have to pay for her.'

'Will I?' He looks worried.

'Zac! Of course you will! It's your first date!'

He looks relieved. 'Do I just pay on the first date then?'

'I don't know! Work it out with Rommy. Sorry, Rom-ill-lee. I'm going to phone her!'

'Don't say anything!'

'As if I would!'

Rommy's even more excited than Zac. When I ring her, she's positively ecstatic.

'Thank you! Thank you! Thank you!'

'What for?'

'You know . . .'

'No I don't.'

'Eva! He's asked me out; Zac's actually asked me out!'

'Has he?'

'You knew, I can tell! You helped to set this up!'

'No I didn't.'

'Yes you did! Don't pretend.'

'I didn't, you dope.'

'I don't mind, honest. I'm not daft. Pretending not to want to talk to me! What a brilliant idea! Oh heck!' Her tone changes. 'Do you think he's only asked me out because he feels sorry for me?'

'Yeah, right. Nothing to do with the fact that you've got a figure to die for and you're drop-dead gorgeous, he just feels sorry for you.'

She giggles. 'I can't believe it, I've fancied him for ages.'

'Never! Who'd have guessed?'

'Was I too obvious?' Her voice is worried.

'Just a bit. Never mind, something tells me he's been lusting after you too.'

'Do you think so? Oh, Eva, isn't it great? My first boyfriend . . . maybe my one and only boyfriend . . . and it's my best friend's brother! I can't believe it!'

I hold the phone away from my ear in mock horror. What is she on? She hasn't even been on a date yet and she's marching him up the aisle already. I'd better warn Zac. I can hear her voice, high and reedy, babbling away feverishly.

'Eva? Evie! Are you there?' She's stopped at last to pause for breath.

'What?'

'Are you OK with this?'

'Yeah, 'course I am.'

'Really?'

'Really.'

For once, I'm telling the truth. I *am* OK with this, surprisingly, because not so long ago I wasn't too sure about my brother and my best mate having the hots for each other. But things are different now. This can work to my advantage.

You see, if Rommy's going out with Zac, I'll know where she is, won't I? And, what's more important, I'll know who she's with.

Because, if she's with Zac, Doughnut can't get her sweet, sticky mitts on her, can she?

And now my mother's abandoned me, and my big sister's not around any more, I need my best friend, more than ever.

Nobody told me what had happened to Amber. I guess they thought I had enough to contend with, what with cuts to the face and mouth, two broken ribs, contusions to the chest, severe concussion and bruising to the brain. Oh, and one pink lunchbox, smashed to smithereens. Poor little Eva.

Dad and Ben took it in turns to sit by my bed. I was out of it for the first few days, then when I came round I was hurting and all I did was cry for Mum. But she was with Amber, refusing to leave her bedside for a minute. I just remember being sore and crying a lot and wondering where Mum was. When they told me she was with Amber, I cried even more.

After a while they moved me into the general ward next to Zac. His head was cut by flying glass from the windscreen and he wore a bandage round it, like a war-hero, and his broken arm was plastered and in a sling. I was jealous because I'd always wanted to wear a sling. It wasn't fair, my ribs were broken, they'd said they were, but they didn't even bother to put them in plaster, they just strapped them up with bandages that were too tight and they huu-rrt, they really did!

I was miserable all the time I was in hospital. My mouth was sore and I couldn't eat even though I was hungry, and Ben and Dad were useless at cheering me up. They didn't even try, they just sat at my bedside looking sad. Then the day arrived at last when Mum came to see Zac and me. She didn't look like Mum any more, she was white-faced like a ghost and she was bandaged up too, round her head and hands, but it was more than that, or less than that perhaps, because it was like she wasn't all there, like part of her was missing. She hugged Zac as if she'd never let him go but when she wrapped her arms round me I screamed because my ribs and chest hurt so she sat there trying to hold my hand instead with her poor, bandaged mitt, tears pouring down her face.

Then she left me again. She went back to Amber, I suppose.

It's worked. Rommy and I are firm bezzies again. Now they've been on their first date (don't ask, I could tell you all about it in minute detail but, believe me, you don't

138

want to know), she's officially going out with Zac and dreaming of becoming my sister-in-law. She hangs about with me all the time jawing about him. Everyone else is bored to tears (so am I!) and has the sense to keep their distance, except for Doughnut who still hovers around in our personal space like a pestering giant cranefly. But Rommy hardly notices her now that her sole topic of conversation is Zachary Jamieson.

'What's his middle name, Eva?' She's busy adorning her school bag with highly original inscriptions such as ROMMY4ZAC and RLZ4EVER. On her left arm she's drawn an ornate heart of red flowers with ZAC in the middle in black indelible ink. It's quite impressive.

'Go and ask him.'

'I can't, he's playing football. He won't want me hanging around, asking him personal questions.'

'Yes he will,' giggles Doughnut annoyingly. I silence her with a look.

'No, you're right, he won't. It's Alan, like my dad. What's your mum going to say about your arm?'

She examines it proudly. 'Good, innit? She's not going to see it.'

'Bet she will, she'll go spare. Mine would.'

'How *is* your mum, Eve?'

I stiffen and dart a quick look at her as she starts carefully inking his name yet again on her bag, her perfect white teeth biting the tip of her pink tongue in concentration. How much does she know now she's become a newly elected, honorary member of our family?

'All right.'

She doesn't react, more interested in writing my brother's name with long swirls and curlicues. (*Curlicue: decorated curls and twists* – a lovely word, it sounds just like its meaning.) I relax. She's just being polite. Let's face it, Zac's not going to tell her Mum's been carted off to the funny farm, is he? I mean, I don't think that's the sort of thing you'd discuss on your first date, not that I've been on one. Yet.

I don't know if she *is* in the funny farm to be honest. I'm exaggerating as usual. Officially, she's on a residential counselling course, 'wrestling with her personal demons', Dad said. Personally, I think that sounds just as bad, like she's an alcoholic or a druggy and is in rehab, instead of being just a normal person who gets a bit down sometimes.

I wish she'd get back up again and finish those demons off and come home to us, where she belongs.

'There!' says Rommy triumphantly, sitting back on her heels to scrutinize her latest work of art. 'What do you think?'

'Lovely,' says Doughnut automatically before she's

even looked at it. Me, I'm a bit more critical. This one is the most ornate yet, but unless Rommy's literally gone loopy with love, she's made one whopping mistake. 'Who's Zaj?'

'It's Z–A–J,' she spells. 'Zachary Alan Jamieson. Zaj. I like it, it's cool. Maybe I'll call him that from now on. It can be my own special name for him.'

'It can be my own special name for him,' I mock in a falsetto voice. She's not only saying my brother's name a billion times a day and graffiti-ing it on every available surface including her own body, she's making up new ones for him now. Doughnut, who's sitting next to us, hanging on to Rommy's every word, giggles complicitly at me. I frown.

'What's your middle name, Eva?' asks Rommy, ignoring my silly voice. I raise my eyes to heaven in disbelief. Excuse me? You know this already, Romilly Stevens, you're just unable to retain any information that doesn't revolve around Zachary Alan Jamieson.

'Elizabeth, remember? I'm named after both my grandmothers.'

'E-E-J,' spells Rommy thoughtfully. 'Eej. Hmm. Not as nice as Zaj.'

For goodness' sake! My eyes start to disappear celestially again but they shoot back down to earth as Doughnut sits up and says delightedly, 'Same as me!'

'Pardon?'

She beams at me. 'My middle name is Elizabeth too. It's my mother's name.'

'Well I never, what a coincidence!' I stare at her open-jawed, in mock disbelief. It's a name for goodness' sake, it's not as if we've suddenly discovered we were identical twins, separated at birth. She grins at me idiotically, unsure whether I'm sending her up or not. I scowl back and put her out of her uncertainty.

'Patrice Elizabeth Williams. P-E-W,' spells Rommy, one-track-minding in her own oblivious way. 'Not so good.'

'POO!' I yell in delight. 'Brilliant! Her name is Poo!'

Doughnut flushes an ugly shade of red and sits heavily back on her heels. She reminds me of a timid rabbit who's dared to poke her head above the ground and been blasted to pieces for her bravery, but I can't stop.

'It can be our own special name for her!' My voice is silly and high again, mimicking Rommy's.

'Eva!' Rommy glares at me, stony-eyed with disapproval. 'Stop it!'

'It's OK,' I say, giggling uncontrollably. 'We won't call her that. Doughnut suits her much better. But Poo! It's so funny.'

I'm off again, my laughter pealing out hysterically now, making people sit up and take notice. Suddenly

Doughnut, aka Patty, gets up and stalks off.

'Eva, you're being horrible!' gasps Rommy. 'Now look what you've done!'

'I was only joking,' I splutter. The look of dislike on her face is more than enough to bring me sharply to my senses, but it's her actual words that shock me back to sanity like a bucket of cold water thrown in my face. Not 'Eva, you're being horrible,' not those words, because I know I am, I don't need her to tell me that. I'm being cruel and stupid and very, very childish as well. It's when she says, 'Now look what you've done!'

They're the worst words in the world. They haunt me. They're what Mum said, you see, more or less. Then the car crashed.

There's a dreadful noise coming from somewhere, someone's howling like a banshee, then it mutates gradually into a tortured, ragged sobbing. I'm surprised to discover it's coming from me. My body is racked with convulsions and the tears are pouring down my cheeks.

Rommy is staring at me, her eyes round with fear. Poor thing, she can't tell if I'm laughing or crying.

I can't either.

I've done it again.

This time I meant it, I meant every brutal word I said to Patty. I wanted to hurt her. I'm wicked.

But not Amber. I never meant to hurt her, honest I didn't, that's the awful thing.

It was still my fault though. Mum said it was.

'If I crash this car,' she said, 'it'll be all your fault.'

In the end, when I've calmed down and dried my tears and the few interested onlookers who've come up to see what all the fuss was about have melted away, Rommy and I have a good talk. I thought she'd have rushed off to see to Doughnut's injured feelings, but she doesn't, she seems far more concerned about me.

She knows about Mum. Zac's told her she's gone away for counselling.

'Why didn't you tell me?' she asks.

'You always had the others hanging about. Especially Doughnut.'

'I'm sorry.'

'She's not locked up,' I say quickly. 'She's not mental!'

'Of course she isn't!' she says soothingly, but I bet she thinks she is. 'Is that why you got so upset?'

I shrug, plucking blades of grass, feeling stupid now. 'Maybe I'm just psycho.'

'Don't be daft.'

Her kindness makes me afraid I'll cry again, so I say fiercely, 'You think I'm evil, don't you?'

'No I don't.' She strokes my arm. Rommy's so nice, she

can never bear to see anyone upset. She even sat by Smellody Melody on the bus when we were going on a trip last summer because Warty Graham was away and nobody else would. 'Nobody thinks you're evil.'

'Doughnut does. She hates me.'

Rommy looks uncomfortable. It's true, I think in surprise. Doughnut really does hate me.

'What do you expect? You're always having a go at her, Evie.'

'I'm only having a laugh! She never takes a joke, she always thinks I'm getting at her.' (Because I am, I add to myself, but wisely refrain from saying this aloud.)

'She doesn't understand your sense of humour like I do,' Rommy explains patiently. 'Wait till she gets to know you better, then you'll get on like a house on fire.'

I wish she would disappear in a cloud of smoke. 'She doesn't want to get to know me better, she just wants to be friends with you,' I say glumly, truthful for once.

Rommy's face brims over with sympathy. 'You've just got off to a bad start.'

I can't bear her pity. What is it with me? Why don't I mind people feeling sorry for me if I'm lying, but if I'm telling the truth I hate it? It's one thing me making out that Patty Williams loathes me, but when Rommy agrees, it freaks me out. I say savagely, honest for once, exposing my biggest fear, 'She just wants to take you away from me. She wants you for a best mate.'

'Don't be silly.' Rommy puts her arms round me. 'You're my best mate,' she says earnestly. 'Just be nice to her, Eva. For me?' She squeezes me tight and my eyes close in relief as I hug her back.

'OK,' I say, holding her as if I'll never let her go. 'I'll try.' You see, I know how lucky I am to have Rommy, she's such a good person. Not like me. She'd never, ever, do anything to hurt me, or anyone else for that matter. Not intentionally, anyway.

But I did nick her from Sophie.

So, if I'm not careful, Patty Williams could nick her from me.

To be a top gymnast you should be as strong as an ox, as supple as a yogi, as nimble as an acrobat and as delightful to watch as a dancer. You must be capable of performing the most complicated and potentially dangerous moves accurately and make them look easy and aesthetically pleasing. Gymnastics requires huge discipline and a colossal amount of training but reaps enormous benefits. Scientific tests have shown that world-class gymnasts are fitter than virtually any other kind of sportsman (or woman).

I'm curled up on my bed, my nose deep in a book I've taken from the shelf in Amber's room. The house is quiet, dead. It never used to be like this. Zac's around somewhere, but goodness knows where Ben is, I never see him any more. He's either out with his mates or he's in bed, nursing a hangover. Rugby training's finished for the summer and he's supposed to be revising for his A levels which start soon, but he doesn't seem to be making much of an effort. Come home, Mum, we need you. This family's falling apart. I'm surprised Dad's not on his case, but he doesn't appear to have noticed, too busy working or running or having a drink himself. He's often late home now and I have wondered once or twice whether he's been to visit Mum, but he hasn't said. He would have told me, wouldn't he?

I sigh and shift my weight. The book is heavy and old, and it's full of pictures of gymnasts like the tiny Russian Olga Korbut, who never became Olympic champion but who changed the face of gymnastics overnight with her bubbly personality, and the Romanian Nadia Comaneci. I suspect it belonged to Mum first, but the sentiments haven't changed. No wonder so many young girls dream of becoming the next Comaneci. She was the fourteen-year-old legend who became the first Olympic gymnast to score a perfect 10, back in 1976. 'Little Miss Perfect', she was known as.

My mum must have been about my age then. I remember once, she told me how she watched spellbound, glued to the telly, as Little Miss Perfect leapt, tumbled and danced her way to victory in Montreal.

'I was dead sporty in those days,' she'd said wistfully. 'I was dying to join a gym club so I could score the perfect 10 too but there was nothing around. I could've been good, you know.'

Lucky for her, she had Amber instead to make her dreams come true. Our whole family life revolved around gymnastics. The boys didn't do it – Ben was already into rugby and Zac's very first steps were taken in hot pursuit of a football, so legend holds – but gymnastics training was so intense and Amber climbed up the competition ladder so quickly, our family timetable was organized around gym sessions. And because Mum helped out there (so she could keep an eye on Amber's progress and give it a prod if necessary) and I had to tag along with her, I kind of grew up assuming that gym was an inescapable part of life, like school, something that you had no choice about, you just had to do.

I raise my eyes from the book. Was there ever a time I contemplated giving it up? Not really, I'm too competitive. Looking back, I wasn't like Amber, I wasn't amazing, but I was OK and, of course, I wanted to be as good as Amber one day. She was both my role model and my biggest rival rolled into one. I spent so much time in the gym over the years, doing my own sessions, then joining in with the older groups while I hung about waiting for Mum and Amber that, eventually, I became a good gymnast in my own right.

But, if I'm honest, nowhere near as good as Amber.

I suppose the natural time for me to stop would have been when I went to secondary school. That's when most girls give up, around puberty, when their bodies develop lumps and bumps that get in the way of moves they found easy when they were pre-pubescent. Aren't they horrible-sounding words by the way? *(Puberty: being or becoming functionally capable of procreation through natural development of reproductive organs; pubescence: arrival at puberty; pubes: lower part of abdomen covered with hair, at and after puberty.)* Oh please! Spare me the details!

Anyway, that's about the time other things become important like music and clothes and boys and going out, and it often coincides with when the penny drops for most gymnasts that, actually, they're never going to be a second Nadia Comaneci after all.

But that was never an option for me. I couldn't have stopped then, even if I'd wanted to. My life was already mapped out. Lucky for Mum she had me as well as Amber. BOGOF, that's what they should have called me. Buy one, get one free. I had to go on and win all those trophies for Mum that Amber wasn't going to walk away with any more.

Let's face it, Amber wasn't going to walk anywhere.

Don't get me wrong, Mum never told me I had to do this. She wouldn't.

Amber did though.

It was all my fault you see.

★ ★ ★

'Aren't you going to gym tonight?' Zac's standing at the door of my bedroom, eating a bag of crisps.

'What time is it? Oh flip. Dad? Dad! Can I have a lift?'

'He's gone out for a run.'

'I'm going to be late! I haven't had any tea, it's not fair.' I leap off the bed, grabbing my bag from the floor where I'd dropped it the night before.

'Have a crisp.' Zac shoves the packet beneath my nose. I brush it away irritably.

'Salt, fat and E numbers? Not for me, sunshine.'

'You're turning into Mum.'

'Thanks. Have you seen my trainers?'

'Nope,' he says helpfully. 'You're getting skinny.'

'No I'm not.' I stop for a second and examine myself in my full-length mirror, turning sideways, automatically standing tall and sucking my belly in till it disappears beneath my ribcage. Then I breathe out and my belly pops back into place again. 'Yuk, look at that,' I say, grabbing it between my fingers.

'Anorexic.' Zac nods sagely. 'You'll be puking your breakfast up in the toilet next.'

'That's bulimic, ignorant. I'm not bulimic and I'm not anorexic, I just never get a minute to eat.'

That's not strictly true. I've been lying on my bed with my head in a book for the past hour when I suppose I could have been making myself something healthy to eat.

The thing is, I've been brought up to view fast food as the devil's own. I'd be more scared of being caught eating a Big Mac than being found smoking or taking Class A drugs or in flagrante (and if you don't know what *that* means, look it up).

But the trouble is, the sort of good, wholesome, nourishing food that Mum's brought us up to eat – well it's not fast food, it's slow food. It takes ages to prepare and ages to cook. I mean, I do try. Take last night for instance. In a mistaken burst of goodwill, I thought I'd cook supper for everyone.

'What are you making?' asked Dad, poking his head around the door as I bashed around in the kitchen, assembling all the ingredients.

'Mum's Lentil and Mediterranean Vegetable Salad with Goat's Cheese.'

'Oh good,' he said, his face lighting up, 'we haven't had that for ages. Amber's favourite, if I remember rightly. Got everything you need?'

'More or less.'

I'd looked it up in the recipe book and it looked quite easy. I'd managed to cobble together most of the ingredients. Well not the goat's cheese, obviously, we didn't have any of that lurking in our fridge, but I'd grated a pile of Tesco's Cheddar which would do nicely instead. Not the Mediterranean vegetables either as it turned out, but I'd located a packet of frozen peas, carrots and broccoli in the bottom of the freezer and emptied it into a wok full of hot oil. I'd found a bag of lentils at the back of the cupboard too, that was the main thing.

'Do you know what you're doing?' asked Zac who'd wandered into the kitchen, honing in on the possibility of food like a metal detector searching for coins buried in the sand.

''Course I do!' I said scornfully, swirling the veg round with a wooden spoon.

He picked up the bag of lentils and started scrutinizing the side.

'It says you've got to soak these overnight first.'

I snatched the packet from his hand and read the instructions angrily.

'Damn, how stupid is that? We're hungry now, not tomorrow morning.'

'I'm not eating lentils for breakfast!' said Zac in alarm.

I stared at the pan. The vegetables had started to brown and a thin plume of smoke was rising from them. I jabbed at a carrot with the spoon and it turned itself over in distress. Its underside was black. The smoke alarm started to shriek.

'Eva? Is everything all right?' said Dad worriedly.

'Yes!' I snapped. 'Go away! I told you, I know what I'm doing!'

'Well, if you're sure . . .' Dad grabbed a tea towel and waved it under the alarm till it stopped wailing, then sort of manhandled Zac towards the door. 'Give us a shout if you need a hand.'

'I'm not eating it,' I heard Zac mumbling under his breath as he left the kitchen. I kicked the door shut after him which was a mistake because the alarm started screeching again. Viciously I tugged at the brown paper bag. It split open and lentils flew everywhere. Swearing loudly I bunged the remainder into the pan. Hot oil spat spitefully over my hand.

'Ouch!' I said, grabbing the spoon to stir the lentils into the vegetables but they stuck mutinously to the bottom of the pan. I seized the plate of grated cheese and emptied it over the mass of scorched vegetables, hoping to lubricate the whole smoking mess, belatedly turning the gas down. Dad rushed in to wave the tea towel again, slipped on the spilt lentils, said a very rude word and shut up when he saw my face.

'It'll be fine,' I muttered between clenched teeth, brushing my hair out of my eyes.

It wasn't. Not even after Dad stuck the pan under the tap and poured cold water over it. He put it back on the burner then to warm up again and he managed to scrape most of the lentils off the base of the pan but it was no good, they were still hard as bullets and there were too many floaty black bits to get rid of.

'Never mind, Eva, at least you tried,' he said and went off to get us Chinese while I piled the whole lot in the bin. And I thought that was really nice of him but then he spoilt it all later because he had a go at me for not eating enough and went on about how it had cost him a fortune feeding us since Mum's been away. It wasn't my fault I only wanted a few prawns. I mean, I know the calorific value of most of these Chinese dishes and it's not good news, I can tell you. Anyway, I don't know what he was grumbling about; it meant there was more for him and the boys.

Anyway, after last night's fiasco, perhaps it's just as well if I stay out of the kitchen. It still reeks of burnt food, it turns my stomach. The trouble is, I'm not like Mum, I don't think ahead. Well. I do a bit, but not as much as she does.

Actually, I wouldn't want to be like Mum. She's a real worry-guts. Sees danger lurking round every corner.

Not surprising really.

By the time Dad comes home tonight, all hot and sweaty from his run and looking forward to getting in the shower, not driving his daughter to gym club, I've

155

had an apple which is enough to keep me going. I don't know whether I'm losing my appetite or what, but I don't seem quite so hungry nowadays.

I'm not as late as I feared. As we pull up I see Patty going up the steps and Rommy walking across the car park. I'm just about to call to Rommy when I hear her yell, 'Doughnut! Wait for me!' and she breaks into a run. I can't help grinning to myself. My name for her has really stuck. Patty turns and waves and waits obediently for her, door held open wide, and Rommy waltzes through in front of her. Patty follows and the door swings shut behind them.

'Don't forget to pick me up, Dad,' I remind him, slamming the door behind me.

'Can't you get a lift?' he grumbles, his head through the open window.

'No! It's too late to organize!'

'All right, keep your hair on,' he says resignedly. 'I'll be here.'

A car starts up beside me as I cross the car park and I glance involuntarily at the driver who pauses to let me past. It's the nice woman who looked after me the other night, the one with the toffees who was kind and calm, but she doesn't look kind and calm today, she looks cross and disgruntled. (If you're dis-gruntled when you're feeling grumpy, are you gruntled when you're feeling happy? As in, I'm feeling really gruntled today?) I wave at her as I catch her eye.

To my surprise she stops the engine and winds down the window.

'Hello,' she says and smiles up at me. 'How are you?'

'Fine.' I smile back. 'I'm fine now.'

'Good.' Her face becomes serious again. 'Are you going in to gym?'

'Yes.'

'Do you know the girl who went in just now?'

'Patty?' I ask. Instinct stops me from saying Doughnut. 'Patty Williams?'

'Not her,' she says. 'The other one.'

'Rommy. Romilly Stevens.'

'So that's her name, Romilly Stevens.' She shakes her head and frowns. 'Vicious little madam.'

'Rommy?' I stare at her, taken aback. Rommy vicious? No way. Daft, giddy, the concentration of a butterfly, boringly besotted with my brother, but vicious? Definitely not. She's the kindest person I know.

'Did you hear what she called her? *Doughnut*. How spiteful is that?'

'She didn't mean it. It's just a nickname,' I protest, horrified.

'She meant it all right. I knew Patty was being bullied by someone. She hasn't said, but I can tell. It's happened

157

before you see, it's her weight. Some girls can be so nasty.' Her voice is bitter.

My stomach lurches. Patty Williams's mother. She's glaring at me and I'm scared she's going to have a go at me too. A red-hot fire ignites and blazes out of control in my cheeks.

'Oh dear. It's happened to you, hasn't it?' Her tone is gentle again. 'I should have realized. That's why you were upset the other night.' I can't look at her. A wave of sickness threatens to engulf me and I stare desperately at my trainers, willing them to take me away from her, but they remain rooted to the ground. 'Oh!' she cries, in frustration. 'The little vixen! I feel like going in there and having it out with that Romilly Stevens.'

'No! Don't do that! Please!'

She stops, surprised by my vehemence.

'That's not the way to handle it. She . . . she probably doesn't even know she's doing it.'

'Then someone should point it out to her!' She takes a deep breath. 'Or maybe I should have a word with the coaches.'

'No, don't! It'll stop, I promise. Just wait a bit, see what happens, yeah?'

'If you're sure . . .' She sounds doubtful.

I nod eagerly. 'It's better this way. Believe me, I know. It's better not to get parents or coaches involved.'

'Perhaps you're right. And Patty wouldn't thank me, that's for sure.' Suddenly she sticks her hand out of the window and grasps my hand. 'You're a sweet, kind girl. Your mother must be very proud of you.'

How could one person be wrong on so many counts? I snatch my hand away as if I'm burnt. 'Look, it'll be fine, trust me. I'm late, I've got to go . . .'

'Of course. I'm so grateful, thank you so much . . .'

I back away slowly, my legs heavy, trapped by the ball and chain of her indebtedness. This is my dream, my recurring nightmare. I'm desperate to get away.

'Wait!' she calls. 'I don't even know your name!' I turn away blindly, forcing my legs to move, and at last, freed from her worried, grateful eyes, I make my escape.

In the gym everyone is busy. I'm shaking. I can't believe I did that, let that woman think that Rommy was bullying Doughnut. Rommy, of all people! She hasn't got a mean bone in her body. I look around for her. She's standing by the beam with the others, watching Mike spotting Doughnut while she does a flick. (Spotting means he's letting her do it on her own but he's ready to catch her if necessary.) When she pulls it off Rommy cheers and claps and everyone else joins in. Doughnut smiles and Mike pats her on the shoulder. A wave of jealousy automatically surges from the pit of my stomach, as bitter as bile, but I suppress it. Eva, you mustn't do this any more.

Mike catches sight of me. 'Come on, Eva, you're late,' he says, but he's not angry. He knows it's difficult with Mum away.

Rommy beams at me. 'Patty did a flick on the beam!'

'Well done.' I can't look Rommy in the eye.

'Thanks.' Patty sounds startled.

'Somersaults next,' says Mike.

'Does she need those yet?' I say in surprise.

'She will if I put her in for the 4-Piece.'

There's a moment's silence then Rommy, Hannah and Sophie start leaping up and down and clapping and squealing like stuck pigs. Patty looks as astonished as I feel.

'She's not ready for that yet!'

'No, but the rate she's going, she soon will be. Don't look so shocked, I know what I'm doing!' Mike looks at me as if he's amused. I don't know what to say. Suddenly his voice softens and he says, 'She's going to need a bit of help on the bars, Eva. You could give her a hand with that.'

I nod blindly. I can't believe it. I've been doing gym since I was five and she waltzes in, hasn't been doing it for two minutes, and gets put in the same team as me. She's not *that* good.

Is she?

'What about the floor?'

'She'll be fine with that. Needs a lot of polishing up of course, but we'll get there. We'll keep her routine as simple as we can.'

'No, I mean me. What about me? You said I could learn a new move for the next competition.'

Mike's eyes crinkle and he leans over and musses my hair up. 'It's OK, Madam Jamieson, I haven't forgotten. You're not the only one around here you know.'

'I know that . . .' My voice tails away. He's not listening any more. Not the only one! Me? You must be joking. No one else gets a look-in since Patty Pain-in the-neck Williams arrived on the scene. I bite my lip to stop myself from saying something I'll regret.

'Come on, Prima Donna,' says Mike, making his way to the asymmetric bars. 'Come and show Patty what you're made of.'

'Her name's Doughnut,' I say sulkily, following them over.

'What?' Mike turns round startled. 'What did you call her?'

'Nothing.'

The Jimmies fall silent. Then Rommy says uneasily, 'We call her Doughnut. After the doughnut-eating competition. It's a nickname.'

'Do you?' Mike stares at Rommy perplexed and then scans a look at us all before his eyes come back to rest on Patty. 'And are you all right with this?'

'Yes!' Patty jumps to Rommy's defence. 'I don't mind. It's . . . funny.'

'Well, if you're sure. Because I won't tolerate name-calling in this gym.'

'No, I like it.' Patty smiles at Rommy who flashes her a look of gratitude.

'Oh well, no accounting for taste.' Mike shrugs his shoulders and grins. 'Doughnut it is then. Actually,' he adds, 'it's a sign of affection you know, a nickname. It means they like you.'

Patty grins back at him.

'Eva, up on these bars and demonstrate the clear hip to handstand for Doughnut,' he says. It doesn't sound funny any more, it sounds nice.

I wish I had a nickname.

So much for me learning a new move. I spend the whole session working with Doughnut, demonstrating my skills. We have to go back to basics, this is one apparatus she's not good at. Wrong shape I'm afraid. You need a six-pack to be any good at bar work. She can't even get on it properly.

Mike takes no prisoners. 'No!' he yells when her knees hit the floor for the umpteenth time. 'Pike when you go under the bar, how many times do I have to tell you? Eva, show her again.'

At last she makes it to front support position on the low bar. Her face is red and she's breathing like she's about to pass out. 'Now, next step, clear hip circles,' says Mike grimly. 'Eva, demonstrate.'

I do as I'm told, swinging my legs and circling the bar with ease. Again and again I demonstrate, as Doughnut struggles to cast her heavy body around the bar. It's strange, I would have thought she'd have more power in her legs than this, but she seems weighed down by her bulk. She's getting there but it's murderously slow. I can see Mike scratching his head with frustration and I smirk to myself as I twirl gracefully round the bar.

In the end Mike calls Donna over. 'Any ideas?' he asks as they watch Doughnut labouring to pull herself up. Donna looks uncomfortable.

'It's a question of build,' she says. 'I don't really know what to suggest.'

Doughnut gives up and falls heavily to the floor. She's knackered, it's obvious. 'Lose weight?' she says brightly, but she looks fed up.

My sentiments exactly. Donna takes a deep breath. 'Well, there's no doubt about it, if you were as light as Eva here, you'd find it a lot easier.' Doughnut looks even more disheartened, if that's possible. 'Have you lost weight, Eva?' Donna adds.

'No.' I jump to the high bar and upstart, circling backwards into front support, cast, and place my feet on the bar, outside my hands. I circle again, pressing my soles hard into the bar, and dismount with a full turn into a stable landing. The two coaches are watching me closely and I salute them, both hands stretched high in the air.

'Perfect,' says Donna approvingly.

'Yes,' says Mike thoughtfully. 'This may be the way to go. Eva, I want you to work with Doughnut, take her under your wing, so to speak. You OK with that?'

My heart sinks, but I shrug my shoulders. 'Suppose so.'

'Don't look so miserable,' he chuckles. 'There's a pay-off. You want to learn a new move, don't you?'

'Yeah!' I wait, holding my breath.

'The Yurchenko. What do you think, Donna?'

'I don't see why not,' she says. 'She's ready for it, I'm sure.'

'OK, we'll go for that. All right with you, Eva?'

'You bet!'

I'm beaming from ear to ear. The Yurchenko was named after a Russian gymnast, Natalia Yurchenko, who was the first one to do it. There are degrees of difficulty but basically it's a round-off on to the springboard, a back-flip on to the vault, followed by one and a half backward somersaults. I remember Amber doing it. No one in the gym can do it now though, not even Jason. And Mike thinks I'm good enough to teach it to me.

'We'll put a few new tumbles in your floor routine too.'

I feel as if I've won the lottery. He's forgotten all about Doughnut. Now she knows what it feels like. She picks her sweatshirt up from the mat and straightens up, her face impassive. 'Can I go now?' she asks.

''Course you can,' he says. 'Now, don't worry about it, you'll get there now you've got Eva looking after you.'

She shrugs. 'Not till I lose weight, I won't.'

Donna smiles at her kindly. 'I've got some information on nutrition in the office. Come with me and I'll see if I can dig it out for you.'

'OK.' She looks behind us and calls, 'Hi, Mum. I won't be a tick.'

She and Donna go off together and Mike and I turn as one. Mrs. Williams is standing watching us from the other side of the gym. Mike raises his hand to her and she returns his wave and comes over to join us. My heart dives.

'How's she doing?' she asks.

'Great!' says Mike cheerfully. 'She's doing great. I'm going to put her in for the county competition if all goes well. She's got a bit of work to do on the bars, but Eva's been giving her a hand with that.'

'Thank you.' She smiles at us both. 'This girl has been such a help to my daughter.'

'Has she?' Mike says in surprise. I feel my colour rising. 'Glad to hear it. She seems to be settling in all right, doesn't she?'

'I'm not sure,' says Mrs Williams, glancing at

me uncomfortably. 'Actually, I think she may be being bullied.'

'Is she?' Mike looks alarmed. 'Surely not.'

'I'm afraid so. Some girl called her an offensive name. I heard it with my own ears, this evening when I dropped her off.'

'Well,' says Mike, 'we can't have that. Can you see the girl here, Mrs Williams?'

'Oh,' she looks uneasy, 'I don't want to get anyone into trouble. I just want it to stop.'

'OK. Can you tell me what she called Patty?'

'Doughnut.'

'Oh, I see.' Mike grins in relief.

It's Mrs Williams's turn to go pink now. 'I know it's just a silly name, but it's unkind.'

'It's not what you think.'

Mike takes her by the arm and lowers his voice, turning them both away from me so I have to strain to hear.

'It's nothing to do with her size, Mrs Williams. It's come from this daft doughnut-eating competition she introduced us to, here in the gym. The girls loved it. They nicknamed her Doughnut after that.'

Patty's mum turns even pinker. 'Oh, I'm so sorry! I didn't realize. How silly of me! I knew I shouldn't have said anything, but you know how you worry about them . . .'

Mike pats her arm comfortingly.

'You were right to bring it to my attention. But you've nothing to worry about, believe me, they're not being nasty. They really like her, you know.'

She nods and turns around and catches me watching them. 'I'm sorry,' she says. 'You were right. I shouldn't have said a word, it was a fuss about nothing. You won't tell Patty, will you?'

I shake my head. Suddenly she leans forward and kisses me lightly on the cheek. 'Patty's so lucky to have a friend like you.'

I mumble something non-committal.

If she only knew what was going on in my head.

I'm not sure *I* do, actually, I'm so mixed up.

For a start, I still feel really bad about letting Rommy take the flak like that for Patty's new name. But the thing is, there's no harm done, is there? I mean, she's never going to find about it. And I'm so glad I'm not in trouble. I mean, *I'm* not a bully; I don't go round beating people up. Calling someone a few names doesn't do anyone any harm, does it? *Sticks and stones may break my bones, but names will never hurt me*, everyone knows that.

I'm really pleased the name Doughnut has stuck, by the way. Like, OK, it might be nice to have a nickname but you wouldn't choose that one, would you? I'm pleased she's no good at bars too and Mike has asked me to help her because now he's noticed me again and, when he teaches me this complicated new move, I can win the county 4-Piece and make Mum happy.

But, on the other hand, I don't *want* to help her get better at gym. Because she could overtake me, couldn't she, if she gets really good, and steal the gold medal? Then Mum is going to be so disappointed and will probably have to go away again to get over it.

And I'm still worried if I'm not careful she'll pinch my best friend from me, whatever Rommy says. '*They really like her*', that's what Mike said. They'd get on so well, Rommy and Doughnut, if they had the chance, I know they would. They're two of a kind, they're both so . . . *nice.*

Not like me. I'm not nice at all.

I just pretend to be.

Dad's late picking me up again. I think he's been to the pub while he waited for me because I can smell beer. Mum would go mad if she thought he was drinking and driving. When we get home the house is in darkness. Dad switches on the lights and calls, 'Ben? Zac?' but there's no reply. He mutters under his breath and goes out to the kitchen, returning with a bottle of red wine, and pours himself a large glass. 'Where is everyone?' he asks, then goes to the foot of the stairs. 'Ben?' he yells. 'Are you up there?' There's no reply. He takes a swig of his wine and collapses into a chair. 'I needed that,' he says and takes another, bigger one, then closes his eyes. Two minutes later, he's fast asleep with the glass, half full, in his hand. I take it from him and go out to the kitchen to throw it away. As I pass through the hall, Zac's letting himself in. He nods at the wine glass.

'When did you take to the bottle?'

I take a sip. It's sour and musty. I spit it back into the glass, immediately. 'Yuk!'

'You're weird. Want a kebab?' He thrusts a polystyrene container in front of my nose. The sight and smell of the burnt, congealed meat, covered in globules of greasy sauce, turns my stomach, and I push it away so quickly it nearly falls on the floor.

'Steady on!' barks Zac.

'It's disgusting! How can you eat garbage like that?'

'All right, calm down. At least I eat.'

'So do I!'

He raises his eyebrows but says nothing, stuffing more dead sheep into his mouth, the grease running down his chin. I turn away, revolted. I wish Mum was here.

That night I'm all churned up and I can't sleep.

In the end, I slip into Amber's room and lie on top of her cold, smooth bedspread in the dark. Before long, it's all coming out, the whole sorry tale, like a vile, suppurating sore that won't stop oozing. I tell her how worried I am about Doughnut, all the stuff about how I let her mum blame poor innocent Rommy for bullying her and, most of all, how scared I am she's going to pinch Rommy *and* the gold medal from me. Amber is silent, you wouldn't know she was there. In the end I have to beg her to say something.

'I'm thinking,' she says finally. 'Give me a chance.'

The sound of her voice reassures me and I snuggle down beside her, prepared to wait. I know she'll have an answer, she always does. As I get used to the gloom I can make out the thin outline of her body under the sheets and can sense rather than hear the soft intake and expulsion of her breath. I feel myself calming down and my mind clearing.

At last she says, 'You need a plan.'

'What sort of plan?'

'First of all, you're never going to put Rommy off Doughnut, she's friendly to everyone.'

'I know,' I say morosely.

'So, you'll have to put Doughnut off Rommy instead.'

'Right.' I consider this for a moment. 'How do I do that?'

'Dunno. That's for you to decide. And secondly, if you want to make sure you win the gold medal in the 4-Piece and you're scared Doughnut's going to beat you, then there's only one sure-fire way.'

'What?'

'Remove the opposition from the equation.'

'What do you mean?'

'Get rid of her,' she intones in a deep, scary voice, the one she adopted for those ghost stories she used to tell me when I was little. No wonder I couldn't sleep! I know she's kidding but I can feel the hairs prickling on the back of my neck.

'How?' I play along with her, intrigued to hear what she comes up with.

'Shoot her.'

I giggle. 'No gun.'

'Set fire to her.'

'Too messy.'

'Put her in a barrel, stick her in the river and see if she drowns. Isn't that what they did to witches in the olden days?'

'She's too fat, I'd never get her in the barrel.'

Amber is shaking with silent laughter beside me.

'Seriously, Amber, what can I do?' I rise up on my elbow and peer at her, just about making her out in the darkness.

She grins wickedly at me. 'Why are you asking me? You're better at getting rid of people than I am.'

'Amber!'

'Well, you asked for it!' She yawns widely, stretching her thin white wrists, almost transparent in the darkness, above her head. 'I've told you already, get her to think Rommy's not as nice as she makes out. Make her believe it's all an act and she's really an evil cow underneath. Then she'll avoid her like the plague, the way she avoids you.'

'Amber! I can't do that!'

'Why not? Her mother thinks so already. You're halfway there.'

'Poor Rommy.'

'She'd never know.'

'I'd never get away with it.'

'You would, you devious little monster!' Her voice is indignant. 'Think about all the times you got me into trouble when you were little!'

She makes it sound like something I should be proud of. In spite of myself, I chuckle.

'You get to keep your best friend that way,' she whispers persuasively. 'Go on, use your imagination.'

My mind races ahead, fuelled by Amber's mischief-making, seeing possibilities.

'Well, MAYBE, at the same time *I* could pretend to befriend Patty! Like, if I give her a hand in the gym like Mike suggested, I can keep an eye on her, can't I? See how good she's getting.'

'Now you're talking!' Amber's eyes shine with excitement. 'You can bring her down a peg or two that way if you need to, undermine her a bit . . .'

'. . . in the nicest possible way of course.' We giggle, united in our devilry.

'What you've got to do is turn her against Rommy gradually,' she continues insidiously, prodding me further along the path of no return. 'Drip-feed Doughnut nasties about her.'

'OK.'

'Go on then, make a start.'

'What, now?'

'Yes! No time like the present.'

'Amber! It's past midnight!'

'The witching hour!' Her eyes glint at me, goading. 'Send her a text, I dare you!'

I jump up and run into my bedroom. My phone is on the floor beside my bed. I grab it and text the words:

```
Rommy! You are so mean! Donut's not so bad
when you get to know her. She can't help
being overweight. xxx
```

Then I tap in Doughnut's number and press send before I have time to change my mind.

Done it! I go back to Amber's doorway, my phone in my hand, and stand there, peering in. I can just make her out in bed, her body an indefinable shape in the bed, like a sand-dune in the desert.

'I've done it,' I say triumphantly.

'Good.'

'Do you want to see what I wrote?'

'Not really. I'm cold.' She shivers and turns away from

me, losing interest now the deed is done, pulling the bedclothes tight round her neck, and wriggling further down in the bed until she's practically invisible. You'd hardly know she was there. My satisfaction evaporates.

'You're a fat lot of use . . .' I grumble.

'What do you expect?' says Amber. Her voice fades away, grumpy with weariness. 'I'm tired. Why can't you leave me in peace?'

Downstairs I hear the front door open and Dad's voice yelling, 'And where the hell do you think you've been to till this hour? Do you know what time it is?'

Ben's voice answers, sounding slurred. I close Amber's door behind me silently and make my way in the darkness, past Mum's and Dad's empty room, to my own cold bed.

'Eva! I can see your ribs!'

We're changing after netball and I'm reaching up to get my shirt from the hooks above the benches when Sophie's strident tones makes everyone turn and look at me.

'So?'

'You're skinny.'

'No, I'm not.' I button my shirt up and fasten my tie loosely round it, pulling the knot carefully down to the third button from the top. I can feel everyone taking a furtive peek at me but, to be honest, I'm more concerned that they'll notice my crumpled shirt which I didn't have time to iron this morning.

'Eva's got a lovely figure,' pipes up Rommy loyally. 'Don't you think so, Doughnut?'

Next to her, Doughnut mumbles something indistinct and carries on struggling to do up her skirt.

'It's all that running she does,' carries on Rommy,

oblivious. 'I need to lose weight, I'm getting fat.' She pulls the waist of her skirt down and examines her belly gloomily, a flat plateau framed by the twin rising peaks of her hip-bones.

'Me too.' Sophie swivels round to inspect her neat little bum. 'I've got cellulite.'

'And me,' says Hannah predictably, squeezing her perfectly toned thighs.

'I suppose we could all do with losing a bit,' says Rommy ruefully. 'Except for you, Eva. You've already lost loads.' Beside her, Doughnut stuffs her PE kit in her bag and sits down heavily to take off her trainers.

'Get up early and run to school like I do then.'

Rommy sighs. 'I do try.'

'Yeah, once in a blue moon. What about you, Sophie? I thought you and Hannah were going to run to school?'

'I keep meaning to, but, like I said, I'm not a morning person,' says Sophie shiftily.

'It's so hard to get out of bed in the mornings,' groans Hannah. 'It's a scientific fact, you know, that teenagers need more sleep than adults.'

'I'm a teenager! I don't need a lot of sleep. That's just an excuse.'

'Maybe we should all just go on a diet,' suggests Rommy, anxious to avoid an argument as usual. 'What do you think, Doughnut?'

Doughnut's head is bent over her shoes. The next second, Mrs Ellis booms, 'Get a move on, you lot, you'll be late for your next lesson! Hannah, Sophie, Romilly, what are you waiting for? Eva?'

'Just getting my stuff together, Miss,' I say, cramming my kit in my bag as the other three exit the changing rooms. Next to me, Doughnut straightens up and runs her fingers through her hair. She looks the picture of misery.

'Want to borrow my comb?'

She looks surprised but takes it from me and runs it through her mousy hair. It doesn't look much different. For a second I almost feel sorry for her. Poor Doughnut, she really hasn't got much going for her, has she?

'Thanks.' She hands it back to me delicately, as if she's afraid I'll bite her hand off.

'Don't mind Rommy,' I say, my voice tinged with pretend concern. 'She doesn't mean to keep on at you.'

'What about?' She looks puzzled.

'Being, you know, a bit . . . just a little bit, I mean, honestly, you'd hardly notice . . .'

'Fat?'

'No! No, I wouldn't call you that. I mean, I know I did before, but I didn't really know you then, I was just teasing, honest. But you know what Rommy's like . . .' My voice trails away.

She picks up her bag. 'I'm beginning to,' she says stiffly.

'Come on, we've got maths next. Don't want to get into trouble. Stick with me, kid.' I smile at her blithely and she follows me obediently out of the changing room and along the corridors to the maths block, like a sheep being led to slaughter.

At gym club, the pace is hotting up. Everyone in our session is busy preparing for the 4-Piece. I spend a lot of time working with Mike on the Yurchenko; it's not easy, but I'm getting there. Donna's putting us through our paces on the beam. The rest of the time I work with Doughnut. Not only does Mike coach us together on the bars, using me to demonstrate to Doughnut, but he's working on our floor routines together too. It's got so that now Doughnut waits outside for me to go in. Sometimes her mother waits with her too. I think they're a bit wary of the others, especially Rommy, only neither one is admitting it to the other. Who would have thought a simple text sent to the wrong person by mistake (oops!) would have worked so well!

Poor Rommy. She can't work out why Doughnut's abandoned her.

'She doesn't seem to want to know me any more. What have I done?'

'Nothing, silly.' I give her a squeeze. 'She's a strange one.'

'She is, isn't she? I thought she liked me.' Rommy's brow furrows. 'I can't think of anything I've done to upset her.'

'You haven't,' I say truthfully.

She smiles at me gratefully. 'You're being really nice to her nowadays, Eva.'

'Well,' I shrug, 'it was you who told me to.'

Rommy watches as Doughnut struggles on the bars. 'It's a shame. She'd be so much better if she could get rid of some of that weight round her middle.'

'Tell her,' I say. 'She'll listen to you.'

'Do you think so?' She looks doubtful.

'Rommy, you'd be doing her a favour. That's what friends are for.'

'Well, if you're sure . . . I will if I get the chance.'

I'm working on the bars with Mike when he sends Doughnut off to have a rest. As I run up I notice Rommy squatting down beside her and I dig my feet heavily on to the board, powering myself forward and upwards. I grasp the high bar in a long swing and heave my legs on to the one beneath, pausing for breath, and look down on the pair below. Rommy looks up and waves and they watch as I execute a 360-degree roll.

'Concentrate,' warns Mike and I tear my eyes from the pair of them. He talks me through the sequence we are practising, slowly and clearly, and I circle the bar backwards and wait for his next instruction. Before me now, Rommy is talking animatedly to Doughnut who sits silent and glum. Mike and I work for a while on between bar skills and I focus hard as I lean, pike, hang and rotate myself around the two bars. By the time I dismount, I'm panting hard and Doughnut is nowhere to be seen.

'Well done!' says Mike with a grin. 'You're coming along nicely.'

'Thanks.' I smile at him happily. Praise indeed.

'I did what you said.' Rommy appears at my shoulder. 'I wish I hadn't though.'

'Why?'

'She's gone off in a huff.'

'Oh well, can't be helped,' I say dismissively. 'At least you tried.'

'Take a rest,' says Mike. 'Doughnut's turn. Where is she?'

'Outside.'

'What's she doing out there?' barks Mike. 'She should be in here watching you! She's got a lot to learn.'

'Rommy says she's having a strop.'

Mike shakes his head in disbelief. 'Who's upset her this time?' He turns to Rommy. 'Was it you?'

'No!' says Rommy, but she looks guilty.

Mike frowns. 'I'll have her mother in here next,

complaining about bullying again. What's wrong with you girls? You're supposed to be preparing for a competition, not having a go at each other!'

'I'll get her,' I say quickly. Behind me I hear Mike continuing to rant at Rommy.

'I wish you were all as focused as Eva! She doesn't let silly disputes get in the way of her training. Commitment, that's what we need in this gym, not stupid, childish squabbles . . .'

I smile to myself.

Outside, Doughnut is sitting on the kerb by the main door, her head down. I sit beside her and she kneads her eyes quickly with the heel of her hand and sniffs.

'You OK?' I ask gently.

She hiccups dolefully. What a sight! Her eyes are red and her face is puffier than usual. If I had a tissue, I'd give it to her.

Her mum gave me one when I was crying.

I push the thought away quickly.

'What's up?'

Her normally pleasant face twists into a horrible grimace. 'Rommy.'

'What's she done?'

She makes a noise, a cross between a snort and a sob. 'Nothing.'

'Tell me.'

She shakes her head. I rest my hand on her knee and her eyes fill up again. After a while she sniffs unbecomingly and wipes her eyes with the back of her hand.

'I thought she was my friend.'

'She is,' I say, adding quickly, 'she's friends with everyone.'

'No she's not,' she says shortly. 'She just pretends to be.' Suddenly her face contorts with fury. 'She's been going on at me about my weight.'

'She doesn't mean to be unkind.' I pat her knee consolingly.

'Yes she does.' Her voice is vehement. 'It's OK for her, she's naturally skinny!'

'I know,' I say feelingly. 'It's not fair.'

'You're skinny too.'

'I'm not,' I say automatically then, truthful for once, I add, 'but I have lost a bit recently.'

'Have you?' She raises her head and stares at me with interest. 'How did you manage that?'

Good question. How do I begin to answer it?

Well, if I was truthful I would say, my mum's gone away and I don't know when (if!) she'll be back; I've got no one to cook my meals for me; I forget to eat or I'm too knackered to bother; I kill myself every day, running to and from school; I'm in a perpetual panic that my best friend will go off with someone else; I'm scared to death

I'll fail to win the next gym competition; I lie awake at night plotting how to manage my crazy, mixed-up life; I'm constantly steamed up, stressed out and on edge; and most of all, I live in fear that one day, someone is going to look deep into the darkest recesses of my heart and discover the dreadful, guilty secret that tears me apart, and instead of receding as the years go on, it's getting worse. Worry eats away at you, did you know that? It nibbles you down to your bones.

But I still feel fat.

'Simple,' I say. 'Eat less, exercise more.'

'I'm serious about this,' Doughnut informs me earnestly. 'I'm never going to be skinny, I know that. I wouldn't want to be like one of these supermodels anyway. They've got no flesh on them, they're just skin draped over skeleton . . .'

'Chance'd be a fine thing,' I snort automatically, then remember, too late, my new caring role. Oops! It's OK, she's so fired up, she doesn't notice.

'. . . I just want to be slim and fit. I want to wear little strappy tops and short skirts and fit in a size 10. That would be perfect.'

'You are fit,' I say, more charitably. I'm no good at this nice stuff, but I'm learning.

It's Saturday morning and we're sitting on my bed cross-legged, leafing through fashion magazines. Doughnut and me, weird or what? She flicks pages, searching for the unattainable amongst the flawless, airbrushed, stick-thin perfection of the models who hang the latest high-street must-haves from their emaciated, coat-hanger frames and glower at us from the unreal world of the fashion shoot. Am I jealous? No, actually. They look unreal: strange, pouting phantoms, gaunt and hollow-cheeked, wearing their sadness like the latest designer label. I'm with Doughnut on this one.

We've just finished gym and we're supposed to be looking at gymnastic magazines, but we've got sidetracked. Mike knows the huge catalogue of information Mum's accumulated over the years and he's asked me to look at a move he's been working on with Doughnut this morning for her floor routine, and let her read up about it. Actually, it's amazing how ignorant she is about gymnastics. I guess she started late and she hasn't been immersed in it since birth like me for whom it's as natural as tumbling around in amniotic fluid. (*Amnion: innermost membrane enclosing foetus before birth* – ugh, bad image.) Anyway, she's read it and I've explained to her where she's going wrong. She's a quick learner, I'll say that for her, though it does occur to me, I could tell her anything and she'd believe me. I put her to the test.

'Don't cut out all the sweet stuff, anyway. Chocolate's good, it releases endorphins.'

'Oh good.' She looks up at me. 'That makes things easier. I've got a really sweet tooth.'

'And don't forget to keep up your carbs.'

'Really? I thought they were bad for you.'

'They give you energy. Cakes, biscuits . . . they're not all bad you know.'

She looks puzzled. 'I thought they were . . .'

'Some are,' I retract quickly. She's not as daft as she looks. 'But carrot cake, banana cake, they've got to be good for you, haven't they? They've got fruit in them. Then there's pies and pasties, they're full of meat and veg . . . and potatoes, they're good too.' She looks sceptical. I rush on. 'I love chips, don't you?'

'My favourite.' Her face falls, 'But you know, Eva, they're really bad for you, especially if they're deep-fried. It's the fat content you see.'

'Right.' I nod at her fervently, as if she's just imparted to me the wisdom of Gandhi. 'But you can eat them cooked in other ways and they're just as nice and not fattening at all. Listen! Why don't you stay for lunch? I'll show you what I mean.'

'Are you sure?' Her face lights up, like I'd invited her to go on holiday to Florida with me. 'I'll ring Mum, tell her I'll be a bit late.'

'Baked potatoes,' I say. 'Can't get healthier than that! You make your phone call and chill out up here while I make lunch. I'll call you when it's ready.'

She smiles happily and sticks her thumb up at me.

Outside the bedroom I shake my head in disbelief. She can't be real. From Amber's room, I could swear I hear a snigger.

Downstairs, the kitchen's not looking too bad. Dad had a blitz last night and made us all help. Friday night spent cleaning the house: great start to the weekend! I select the largest potato I can find and a smaller one and bung them both in the microwave. Then I grate a huge piece of cheese and, as an afterthought, open a small can of tuna. When the microwave pings I take out the potatoes, cut open the larger one and plaster it in butter. Then I smother it with the cheese, making sure I pack it down tight first, and continue to pile it on till it's all used up. After that, I add a generous dollop of clotted cream for good measure, stick it back into the microwave until it resembles a melting mountain glacier, then I put it on the table, place a large glass of milk by the side of it, and give Doughnut a call.

'It's ready!'

'Wow!' Her eyes are round with surprise. 'Is that all for me?'

' 'Course it is. Don't worry, it's all good for you. Baked potato – completely non-fattening.'

'Where's yours?'

'Here.' I cut open the smaller potato, inserting a quarter of the tin of tuna into it, and spread it out with a

189

fork till it looks more. Then I pour myself a glass of water and sit down beside her. 'Tuck in!'

'Is that all you're having?' Doughnut looks uncertainly from her plate to mine and back again. 'I'll never eat all this!'

'It's not much. Go on, don't mind me, I had a huge breakfast you see. And I can't eat dairy.'

'Why not?'

'Um . . . allergies,' I say vaguely, then eat a little. 'Yum, this is good. How's yours?' I nibble away at my baked potato, wishing it wasn't quite so dry. 'Oh dear, I hope you like my cooking.'

She forks a kilo of melted cheese into her mouth, devours it and digs in for another. 'Delicious,' she says gamely, and she's off, cutlery flashing, chomping her way through a food mountain of starchy stodge while I poke mine around the plate, trying to make it look as if I'm enjoying it. Eventually she slows down and pushes the plate away.

'I feel sick,' she groans, leaning back in her chair. 'It was really good,' she adds hastily, 'I just ate too much. Aren't you going to finish yours?'

'Later.' I scoop up the remains of my potato, even more unappetizing now it's gone cold, and shovel it in the bin, behind her back. 'Do you want anything else?'

'No thanks, I'm stuffed.' She tugs uncomfortably at the

waistband of her trackie pants. 'I'm not sure all that cheese was good for me.'

'Of course it is. Protein. I eat it all the time.' She doesn't look convinced. I change the subject quickly. 'Right then, do you want to come back upstairs? We could play some music.'

She shakes her head. 'I can't. Mum'll be here in a minute. We're going into town.'

I sit back down at the kitchen table, disappointed in spite of myself. The afternoon stretches ahead, long and empty. I'll be on my own again, Rommy's out with Zac and Hannah and Sophie are doing family stuff. Projecting as much scorn as I can into my voice, I say, 'You're going shopping with your mum? On a Saturday?'

Doughnut colours. 'I know, it's a bit sad, isn't it? I need some new trainers you see, for the competition, and being as Mum's paying . . . We'll probably go for coffee and cake afterwards. More food . . .'

'Sounds like fun,' I say sarcastically, but it doesn't come out like that, it sounds forlorn. I guess I'm really thinking how nice it would be to have my mum around to buy me new trainers and treat me to coffee and cake.

Doughnut nods eagerly. 'Actually, I'm looking forward to it. Mum and I get on great.'

'Great,' I echo, trying this time to inject the right level

of boredom into my tone. Doughnut carries on regardless.

'Yes, we're really close,' she says confidentially. 'There's just the two of us you see.'

'Really?' This sounds a tad more riveting. 'Where's your dad?'

'They got divorced a few years ago, when I was little. I used to think it was my fault.'

'Did you?' I look at her with renewed interest. 'Why?'

'I thought he'd left because I'd been naughty. You do, don't you?'

'What?'

'Blame yourself when things go wrong. You can't help it, you think it's all about you.'

'I suppose so.' Quite an interesting concept, that. I'd have to think about it.

'Is that how you feel?'

'What?' My head jerks back. What does she mean?

'About your mum. Leaving and that.'

'My mum hasn't left us!'

This time she turns a brilliant shade of vermillion.

'Really! Oh no, I'm so sorry! It's just that some of the others were talking and they thought . . . I'm so stupid . . . They thought your mum . . .'

'Well, they thought wrong,' I say indignantly. Cheek! I knew that's what people were thinking! 'She's not run off with someone, she's on a course.'

'I'm sorry!' she wails. 'Rommy said you were going through a difficult time. I just assumed . . . Look, forget I ever said anything.'

Suddenly I see a chance to press home an advantage. Drip-feed her nasties, that's what Amber said. I bristle with righteous anger.

'You can tell them from me, sorry to spoil their fun, but she'll be back home soon and she won't be very happy to hear all these rumours that are zapping around about her. Gossiping crones!'

'I probably got the wrong end of the stick!' She's practically squirming with embarrassment.

'No chance! I know what that lot are like when they get going.'

'They weren't being nasty! They were worried about you.'

'Yeah, right! I bet they were all having a go, Sophie, Hannah and Rommy. Especially Rommy.'

'I can't remember, honest.' Her face is distraught.

'She's supposed to be my best friend!' I post a suitably noble-but-let-down look on my face. 'Be warned!'

'It's just that no one had seen your mum for ages and they were wondering where she was . . . and you were a bit moody . . .' Her voice tails away miserably. 'I'm making it worse, I'd better go. I'm sorry if I've upset you.'

'It's OK. It's not your fault. I'll see you out.'

She follows at my heels into the hall, like a whipped dog. At that moment, the front door opens and Zac comes in, followed by Rommy, laughing and chatting. Timing or what?

'Oh,' says Zac. 'We thought no one was in.'

'Charming!'

'What have you two been up to?' asks Rommy cheerfully.

'Not a lot. We've been looking at gym magazines. Doughnut's just going.'

'Eva made me lunch,' says Doughnut, avoiding Rommy's eyes.

'Blimey, that's a first! Left any for us?' Zac makes for the kitchen. 'Fancy a sandwich, Rom?'

'Doughnut thought Mum had run off and left us,' I say quietly to Rommy. I can feel Doughnut wincing beside me.

'Did she? Oh dear. Have you told her the truth?' Rommy's eyes dart from me to Doughnut and back again.

'I've explained to her that Mum's on a course,' I say warningly.

'Did you know then?' asks Doughnut.

'Yeah, yeah,' says Rommy, picking up my drift. 'Eva told me she was . . . on a course.'

'Why didn't you say when we were all talking about it?'

Rommy shrugs, caught between us both, unsure how much she should impart. It's awkward for a moment, the three of us standing there, but the front doorbell rings and the tension breaks.

'That'll be Mum,' says Doughnut with relief. 'Thanks for lunch, Eva . . . and sorry about, you know.'

'No problem.'

I open the door. Mrs Williams is standing on the step, smiling pleasantly. The smile disappears when she spots Rommy lurking in the background. 'Hello, darling!' she says and gives Doughnut a hug. 'Had a nice time?' Honestly, you'd swear she'd been away for a fortnight. 'Thanks for having her, Eva!' she adds. Doughnut goes down the step and then turns back towards me.

'Why didn't she say anything?' she whispers. I shrug.

'Who knows? That's Rommy for you,' I whisper back. 'You'll get to know her little ways.'

I close the door. When I turn around, Rommy's behind me.

'What was all that about?'

'She was apologizing for eating so much. Don't ever invite her round to your place, whatever you do! She nearly ate us out of house and home.'

Rommy giggles. 'Are you two mates now?'

'Sort of. You told me to be nice to her, remember?'

'EVA!' My brother's voice bellows from the kitchen.

'What?'

'Come here!'

Rommy follows me to the kitchen where Zac's rifling through the fridge. Bread, already buttered, is waiting on the worktop.

'Where's the cheese?'

'Oh dear,' I say, looking contrite. 'I'm afraid it's all gone.'

'You ate it all?' He looks at me blankly.

'Not me! Doughnut.'

'What all of it?'

'Yep, she was hungry. I had to have tuna. There's some left in the fridge, if you want it.'

'Greedy pig!' he says in amazement. 'There was a whole packet there.'

'She is, isn't she? No wonder she's so fat.' I turn to Rommy. 'See what I mean? Looks like she didn't take your advice after all, Rom. Maybe you need to speak to her again.'

Mike decides to concentrate on our floor routines for a while. I'm getting on well with the Yurchenko but Doughnut's still having trouble with the asymmetric bars, so he thinks a change might be in order. I love devising new floor routines. Basically, you've got seventy to ninety seconds to do a sequence of leaps, tumbles and dance to music, incorporating certain required moves. It's got to be smooth and continuous and you lose marks if you stumble or wobble, step out of the floor area or go out of time. I just love it; for me it's the best part of gymnastics. There's nothing quite like the buzz you get from completing the floor successfully and hearing the crowd go mad.

Doughnut is good on the floor.

It's weird because she's so awkward off it. She reminds me of a seal, you know how lumbering they are when they're on dry land, like giant slugs, their heads waving to and fro as they drag their cumbersome bodies slowly down to the sea? Then they slide into the water and change into grey mermaids, sleek beautiful creatures, elegant and graceful, that glide swiftly through the ocean.

Well that's what Doughnut is like. Normally she comes across as being a bit dull and slow, sluggish I suppose, in the true sense of the word. (Well, I am trying to be honest!) But then she walks on to that floor and the music starts and a transformation takes place. She becomes another person, one who's lively and dynamic and light on her feet, who lifts your spirits and makes you want to clap your hands and tap your feet in time to her moves. I saw it at the first competition and I've seen it in the routine Mike is putting together for her now. Everyone in the gym stops and watches her. *I* watch her. She doesn't always get it right, but there's something about her, I don't know what it is, but she's got it.

Amber had it too.

'Eva?' Mike's looking at me curiously. 'Are you OK?'

'Yeah.'

'Your turn now. I want you to practise your Arabian.'

He makes me go over it again and again till I'm pretty near perfect. He's taught me a couple of new tumbles and it's important I'm completely confident with them. Then, when he's satisfied I've got them, he makes me run through the whole routine he's designed for me.

'Good,' he says when I've finished. 'You're getting there. Can you lift your somis this time?'

'I can try,' I say and go through the routine again, trying hard to project more life into them. But my body feels curiously leaden and though I know my somersaults are technically accurate, I can feel they're a bit flat. I can tell by looking at Mike's face he thinks the same.

'Shall I have another go?' I ask, determined to get it right.

'No, take a break,' he says, staring at me thoughtfully with his arms folded. 'Are you tired, Eva?'

'A bit.' I sink down on to the mat gratefully. To tell the truth, I'm exhausted, though I hadn't realized it till Mike asked. Now all I want to do is curl up and go to sleep.

'Are you eating properly?'

'Yeah!'

'You've lost a lot of weight.' He squats down beside me on his haunches.

'No I haven't.' I avoid his eyes.

'*Yes – you – have.*' He speaks slowly, emphatically. There's no arguing with him.

'I needed to.'

'No you didn't, you were perfectly normal. Now look at you. Your leotard's hanging off you.'

'It's old! It's lost its elasticity.'

I can feel him scrutinizing me. At last he says, 'Well,

make sure you don't lose yours or I'll be answering to your mother. When's she home, by the way?'

I shrug. 'Don't know. Soon, I guess.'

He mutters under his breath and stands up. I can't be sure what he said but it sounds like, 'The sooner, the better.'

Doughnut avoids Rommy now like the plague, just as Amber said she would. She doesn't trust her any more. It's quite scary to realize how little you have to say or do to destroy someone's good name.

The downside is Doughnut and I spend more and more time together, now we're working together at gym and Rommy and Zac are glued to each other. Actually, it's not all downside because Doughnut's not so bad when you get to know her, she can be quite funny and she's game for anything. At school, now she's coming out of her shell, she can be a real laugh. Come to think of it, was she ever *in* her shell? That doughnut competition took place not that long after she first arrived on the scene.

Today we have a supply teacher for geography. He's a skinny little guy on the verge of baldness which he tries to cover up by combing what's left of his hair in thin strands across his scalp, and he carries a huge, self-important briefcase, which probably contains nothing but his sandwiches. He looks a bit like a ferret and his name is Mr Minty. You've got to be really good to survive as a supply teacher at our school. You can tell right away, he's got no chance. Dwayne, our resident comedian, seizes on his name immediately with glee and fires off a salvo of jokes about peppermints and humbugs and mints with the hole, and though the poor guy must have heard them a million times before, you can see the ammunition's reached its target. At last, he finally locates the textbooks, with no help from us, and manages to get order.

'Are you a geographer, Sir?' asks Alice, who, unlike the rest of us, is in constant fear she will fail her GCSEs in two years' time if a teacher is away.

'Yes,' he says sharply. You can tell he's lying.

'What's the capital of America?' asks Graham.

'Washington,' he says.

'No it isn't! It's New York,' jeers Graham.

'I think you'll find it's Washington.'

'No way!' says Graham, sticking to his guns. 'It's New York! You see it on the telly all the time.' He turns around to appeal to the class. 'He don't know what he's talking about.'

Everyone laughs at him though no one is at pains to put him right.

'I can assure you I certainly do.' Mr Minty pulls himself

up to his full height of five foot six inches, and looks at Graham as if he'd like to tear him apart with his teeth. What is it with some teachers? '*I can assure you I certainly do!*' Pompous twit! It's like a red rag to a bull.

'Let's see how much he does know then,' yells Dwayne, who actually knows less than zilch himself.

'What's the capital of Russia, Sir?' asks Sophie, joining in the game, on the basis that anything is better than actually having to do some work.

'Moscow,' he says, quick as a flash.

'China?' yells Dwayne.

'Beijing.'

'Australia?' shouts Graham, who seems to be taking an uncharacteristic interest in the lesson.

'Canberra.'

'Wrong!' Graham looks round triumphantly. 'It's Sydney. Everyone knows that. Sydney Opera House.' Beside him, Smellody Melody gazes up at him in admiration.

'Actually,' says the ferret, 'it's Canberra, the seat of government.'

'Hold on, I'll check it,' says Sophie, nipping across to a computer and Googling it. 'He's right,' she declares moodily after a minute. Mr Minty looks pleased with himself.

'Any more?' he says condescendingly. 'Or having

satisfied yourselves that my credentials are, in fact, impeccable, may I suggest we proceed with the lesson?'

'*My credentials are, in fact, impeccable,*' I mimic quietly to Rommy. She giggles.

'You!' he says to me, slamming down the pile of textbooks on my desk. 'Give these out.'

'Please,' I say automatically. He leans over my desk and puts his face close to mine, eyeballing me. His eyelashes are thin and sparse and crusted with sleep and his ferret teeth are yellow and pointy.

'Are you being insolent?' he hisses. His breath is sour and a tiny ball of spittle lands on my cheek. I think I'm going to retch.

'No.'

'No, Sir.'

'No, Sir.'

He straightens up and I wipe my cheek ferociously with the back of my hand, then I get to my feet and start to give out the books. Mr Minty struts around the classroom, his arms clasped behind his back, head held high, as self-important as a ferret can be. The atmosphere has changed in the room, people are tense, waiting, unsure, their eyes glued to their desks. Only Rommy looks at me, anxiously.

'What a pillock,' I whisper to her. It comes out louder than I intended in the now-silent classroom.

'I heard that,' he snaps. 'Collect your detention slip at the end of the lesson.'

I gasp at the injustice of it all. No one else makes a sound. At the back of the classroom, Doughnut suddenly raises her hand. 'Excuse me, Sir,' she says politely. I hate her, toadying up to this vermin.

'What?'

'I have another capital city for you, Sir. I'm sure you won't know it.'

'Oh really?' His eyebrows rise up, searching in vain for his hairline. 'Well, I'm sure I will.'

What is wrong with her? Can't she see no one wants to play any more. No one but the creep himself.

'Right, Sir, you're on. I bet you Eva's detention you don't.'

His eyes glimmer. 'And I bet you, that if I do, you will have a detention too for wasting important lesson time.'

'Yes, Sir. That's fine.'

'Right, I'm ready.' He smiles arrogantly at us all. We sit upright, all eyes on Doughnut, trying to work out her game. She takes her time and when she speaks, her tone is courteous and authoritative, like a quiz-master.

'Here is my question for you, Sir. Please can you tell me what is the capital of the glorious nation of Kazakhstan?'

The whole class explodes. Mr Minty splutters.

'That doesn't count, I'm afraid. It's not a real place.'

'YES IT IS!' we yell.

'I've seen the film,' shouts Graham earnestly.

'Exactly!' says Mr Minty, looking angry. 'It's made up!'

'No it's not,' says Alice, who knows about these things. 'It's a real place.'

'Google it!' suggests Doughnut quietly. There's a mad rush to the computer.

'Sit down!' shouts the ferret but he's lost it. Sophie sits in front of the computer and starts tapping. We all stand around her, waiting with baited breath. At last it scrolls up.

'Astana!' she yells triumphantly. 'Population half a million. It's a proper place all right.'

Everyone cheers.

'Fancy you not knowing that, Sir,' says Dwayne, looking smug.

'Eva doesn't have to do her detention now,' Rommy points out. I beam at Doughnut and she winks at me.

'He don't know what he's talking about!' reiterates Graham.

Alice shares his concern. 'We need a proper geography teacher,' she frets.

Mr Minty never does quite manage to get back control. At the end of the lesson, under threat of keeping us in at breaktime, he does manage to get us reasonably quiet as he writes down our names, having forgotten to take the register at the start. When he comes to Doughnut, she doesn't say Patrice, she says Doughnut and even spells it out helpfully for him when he looks astonished.

'What sort of name is that?' he says scornfully.

'Kazakhstani,' she says, then adds politely, 'Sir.'

Lucky for him the bell goes at that point, though most people don't hear it. It's drowned out by the roars of laughter. Mr Minty does though. He picks up his briefcase and exits the classroom as quickly as he can.

The 4-Piece is getting closer and closer and everyone's becoming nervous. For the first time, we're going to be a five-woman team. Doughnut will officially become a Jimmie. She's more scared than anyone, terrified she's going to let the team down.

'Don't worry about it,' Sophie says, when she's wittering on about it for the nth time. 'Only the first four count anyway for the team medal.'

Nice one, Sophie, the implication being that it will be you, Doughnut, who'll be left trailing behind. I watch as Doughnut's face falls, her self-confidence speared by Sophie's tactlessness.

I'm not so sure Sophie's assumption is correct though.

I've been working closely with Doughnut and I've seen more than the others what she's capable of. She's pretty good and she's improving all the time. The floor's her speciality, though her level of difficulty is nowhere near the rest of us, but she's good on the beam too and she can do a mean half and half vault. It's the bars that let her down: she can manage a clear hip circle with flexed legs now, but she's still got a lot to learn. It's whether she's got enough time, that's the point.

And I don't think Rommy's as committed as she was and I blame my brother for that. Since she's been going out with Zac, I would say her heart's not in it any more. She's even missed some sessions, claiming she wasn't feeling well, but I've noticed they're always the times Zac's been out of the house when I've got home from gym. Hmm, a bad case of Zacharitis, if you ask me. But you can't afford to take time off on the run-up to competitions, it's too intensive.

Actually, I'm not too sure about Sophie and Hannah either. Sophie's always been boy-mad, ever since I met her for the first time in Year 7. It was OK when she had her eye on Jason, our club champion, but since he's made it abundantly clear he's not the remotest bit interested in her (actually, I think he's gay), she's cast her sights elsewhere. Now she's got a crush on a guy in the school footie team (he's gross by the way, I don't know what she sees in him) and she and Hannah hang around him and his friend all day long. It can only be a matter of time till he asks her out or, more likely, she asks him, and then I reckon she'll become a full-on WAG with no time for gym. As it is, the interest is leaking away. Mike knows that, I can hear him having a go at her nearly every session. And as for poor old Hannah, well, she's always been competent, but she never had that much passion in the first place and she'll follow blindly wherever Sophie leads, just as she followed me in the days before I got to know Rommy.

I sigh. It looks to me as if the Jimmies' days are numbered. And Sophie's wrong. I reckon Doughnut could upset the applecart in this competition. Sophie could be in for a nasty surprise.

'You all right?' asks Rommy. I nod. It's been a hard session but it's over now and we're packing up. Doughnut's coming back to sleep at my house tonight. I know, it's weird, but her mum's had to go away for the night and she, her mum, I mean, actually asked me if it was OK if Doughnut stayed over. Well, I could hardly say no, could I? So I've invited Rommy as well, just to keep me sane. You should have seen Doughnut's face when I told her Rommy was staying over too!

Rommy's all excited at the prospect of spending the night under the same roof as Zac. Oh help, I hope they don't get up to anything! I'll have to make sure she sleeps in my bed with me. Doughnut can have Amber's room.

Outside Ben and Zac are waiting for us, by Dad's car. Zac and Rommy fall into each other's arms as though they've been parted for years. 'What are you doing here?' I ask Ben.

'Picking you up, nuisance,' says Ben, twirling Dad's car keys between his fingers. 'Dad's gone for a run.' He looks at Doughnut. 'Aren't you going to introduce me?'

She smiles at him and puts out her hand. 'Hi! I'm Doughnut.'

'Doughnut?'

'It's Kazakhstani,' she says and we all giggle. Ben takes her hand and shakes it.

'I love doughnuts,' he says.

Doughnut's cheeks turn pink but she smiles and her eyes sparkle. 'Me too.'

To my surprise she actually looks pretty. Ben must think so too because he eyes her with interest. She looks different tonight, older; she's still big-framed but today she looks mature rather than lumpy. I think she has lost a bit of weight, despite my machinations. All at once I see her through Ben's eyes and I recognize how much more grown up she is than I am. Beside her I suddenly feel childish, undeveloped, gauche.

'Come on then,' he says. 'Pile in.' He holds the passenger door open and bows to Doughnut, clicking his heels. 'At your service, Ma'am,' he says cheesily. Doughnut seems to find this incredibly funny. I shudder and pile in the back with the two lovebirds. By the time we get home, Rommy and Zac are practically down each other's throats (yuk, double yuk), Doughnut and Ben are chatting away like they've known each other all their lives and I'm feeling as green and hairy as a prize gooseberry.

At home, Dad's back from his run and has actually made an effort and cooked supper for once. It's his speciality, the one I remember from childhood, tuna pasta bake. It's dead easy to make, it just involves opening a few tins of soup, vegetables and tuna, mixing them all up together with some pasta and bunging it in the oven covered in grated cheese and breadcrumbs, but it's always been one of my favourites. Dad ladles big helpings on to our plates but when I smell the baked cheese I feel my stomach turn. The others scoff the lot, but I can't manage more than a few mouthfuls. I can't see why I ever liked it, it just seems like a sloppy, slimy mess to me now, full of additives and chemicals. Dad frowns and says, 'Come on, Eva, stop picking at your food,' and I swish it about on the plate a bit, but when he goes out to the kitchen, Ben and Zac helpfully divide it between them. Dad comes back in with a huge, gooey chocolate cake, shop-bought of course, and everyone's eyes light up, like they hadn't eaten for a fortnight.

'Cake, Eva?' asks Dad, but I say, 'Can't, Dad, I'm stuffed,' and he looks at my empty plate and lets me off.

'Good, more for us,' gloats Zac greedily, cutting himself a mammoth slice. The others follow suit and polish it off between them, greedy pigs. It makes me feel sick, watching them stuffing it into their mouths. Ben insists on Doughnut having the last piece; she'd better not keep on to me again about wanting to lose weight.

Afterwards Zac and Rommy disappear upstairs to listen to music in Zac's bedroom. (Yeah, right!) Doughnut and I watch soaps for a while in the lounge. Ben watches too, suddenly interested in *EastEnders* after all these years for some unknown reason. The phone rings and Dad answers it. After a while he calls me to the phone. 'It's your mum,' he says, holding out the receiver for me. He looks excited. 'She wants to speak to you.' He disappears into the kitchen.

'Hello, you. Hear you've got some friends over for the night.' She sounds relaxed, happy.

'Yeah, Rommy and Doughnut.'

'Doughnut?' she laughs.

'She's new. Mum?'

'Yes.'

'Can she sleep in Amber's room?'

There's silence at the end of the line. At last she gives another little laugh, more brittle this time, and says, 'I don't see why not.'

'Thanks.' I hadn't realized till then I was holding my breath. 'How are you?'

'I'm fine. How's gym?'

'Good. I'm learning the Yurchenko.'

'That's brilliant!' Her voice is light again, animated. 'For the 4-Piece?'

'Yep. And I've got some new tumbles.'

'Wonderful! Won't be long now.'

'Two weeks.'

'I can't wait to see it!'

The penny drops. 'Will you be there?'

'Yes, Eva, I think I will.'

'YAY!!!!'

Dad pops his head round the kitchen door and grins at me.

'When are you coming home?'

'In time for the competition. Got to come and watch you win that gold medal, haven't I?'

'No pressure there then?'

She laughs.

She thinks I'm joking.

Back in the lounge, Dot Cotton is being ignored in the corner while Ben and Doughnut are deep in conversation about some weird band or other. Since when has Ben been into indie music? I don't think so.

'Mum's coming home,' I say to Ben.

He looks up, pleased. 'Wicked.'

I turn to Doughnut. 'Coming upstairs? I'll show you where you're sleeping.'

She gets up obediently and says, 'See you later,' to Ben and follows me out into the hall. As she picks up her bag she spots the cabinet where our cups are on display and stops to gaze at it, rapt. 'You're such a sporting family,' she says admiringly. 'Look at all your trophies!'

'My mum collects them,' I say dismissively.

'I'm not surprised. Is it Ben who plays rugby?'

'Yeah. He's got a scholarship to Oxford because of it.'

'Wow! And Zac's won all these cups for football. And look at all your gym prizes! Cups, medals, awards, there are hundreds of them here! Eva, I had no idea you were so good!'

'I've been doing it for a long time,' I say modestly. 'Come on, I'll show you your room.' I don't want her examining the cups too closely, some of them have got Amber's name on them.

'You're so lucky,' she says wistfully. 'You're good at everything in your family. Your mum and dad must be so proud of you all. Me, I've never won a thing.'

She looks really crestfallen. If I was as soft-hearted as Rommy, I'd be opening the cabinet wide and telling her to take her pick.

Then, out of the blue, I have one of those Eureka

214

moments. It suddenly occurs to me that it makes absolutely no difference whatsoever to Mrs Williams that Doughnut's never won a medal in her life. She's proud of her anyway.

She's the lucky one, not me.

Upstairs, music's pulsating from Zac's room. I put my finger to my lips and lean against the door, placing my ear up against it, and Doughnut follows suit. 'Can't hear a thing,' she whispers.

I nod sagely. 'Must be concentrating hard on the music.'

She giggles and grabs her nose quickly, squeezing it tight to stop herself laughing out loud. Her shoulders are shaking. Suddenly the door opens and we fall inside in an ungainly heap.

'Can I help you?' asks Rommy icily, glaring down at us, hands on hips. Zac's sprawled on his bed, arms behind his head, looking cool and amused. We shriek with laughter and beat a hasty exit. 'Little things . . .' she intones in a bored voice and slams the door shut behind us.

In my room we collapse on the bed, howling our heads off. Doughnut's got this really funny laugh: she stops then all of a sudden it bubbles up again, taking me by surprise, and starts me off again. At last we stop and lie there, getting our breath back as if we've done a five-mile run. Doughnut sits up and looks around with interest.

'Nice room,' she says appreciatively. 'It's huge!'

'Not as big as Amber's,' I say automatically.

'Who's Amber?'

'My sister.'

She looks at me in surprise. 'I didn't know you had a sister!'

I shrug. 'You don't know me that well.'

'How old is she?'

'Um, sixteen. No, seventeen.'

'Don't you know?'

I can feel my colour rising. 'I forget sometimes.'

Doughnut nods understandingly. 'I suppose there are a lot of you, close together. How old's Ben?'

'Eighteen,' I say, glad to change the subject. 'He's off to Oxford after his A levels.'

'He's nice, Ben. So's Zac.' Doughnut's face looks wistful. 'You're so lucky to have brothers and sisters.'

'Sister,' I say, getting off my bed. 'Just the one.' I go down into forward split position, feeling the familiar stretch on my hamstrings. Is it my imagination or are they getting tighter?

'Is *she* good at gym?'

'She used to be.' I stand up briefly then move straight

into sideways splits. They are definitely tighter, especially the right one, where the knee resists lying flat on the floor. Flip, it must be all the running I'm doing, I'll have to watch that. I wiggle into a more comfortable position, then fold myself forward, my stomach flat on the floor, arms stretching out on the carpet.

'Nice,' says Doughnut appreciatively. 'Can I have a go? There's no room to practise in our flat.'

'It's a free country,' I say and get back on the bed to watch her as she goes down easily into sideways splits on the floor. It's surprising how flexible she is, despite her bulk. While she's down there, I show her the swim around exercise we learnt at gym and then I support her while she tries lifting to handstand. She's a good pupil, willing and determined, and it's fun adapting things I've been taught to suit her. An hour later and she can do the complete move.

'Thanks, Eva, for showing me that,' she says finally, collapsing on the bed. 'You're a good teacher.'

'You're a good learner,' I say, flattered.

'I'll ask Mike if I can put it into my routine.'

Suddenly it dawns on me what I've done. I've just successfully taught my rival a difficult move, one which will potentially earn her more points in the competition. Generous or what?

Stupid, more like.

'Am I sleeping here?' she says, bouncing happily on the mattress.

'Don't do that!' I say crossly. 'No, you're in Amber's room. Rommy's in here.'

'Oh,' she says, looking disappointed. 'I've never met Amber before. Won't she mind?'

'She's not here,' I say shortly. 'You've got it to yourself. Come on, I'll show you where it is.'

She picks up her stuff and follows me meekly into Amber's room. 'Wow!' she says, looking round, taking in the neatly arranged medals and posters, books and CDs. 'It's beautiful.' She puts her bag down on the bed then moves it hastily to the floor, smoothing out the satin bedspread. 'And it's all so tidy. I'll be afraid to move in case I spoil anything.'

'She won't be bothered, make yourself at home.'

'If you're sure . . .' She looks around for somewhere to put her sweatshirt, then sits down gingerly on the bed, still grasping it in her hands. 'Is it always as neat as this?' she asks uncertainly.

'Always,' I say firmly. 'Help yourself to what you want. You know where the bathroom is, don't you?'

She nods silently.

'See you in the morning then.'

'OK.' She looks worried, scared almost, as if she knows she shouldn't be there, like a squatter who's afraid of the real owner coming back and turfing her out. At that moment there's a tentative rap on the door and Rommy's face appears around it, lighting up when she sees us.

'So this is where you are! I've been looking for you both.'

'Lover boy let you go, has he?' I declare drily. Rommy ignores me.

'Is this where we're sleeping tonight?' she says eagerly, diving on to the bed, showing none of Doughnut's reticence. 'Amber's room?'

'No, just Doughnut.'

'Aahh, not fair, I love this bedspread.' She pulls it back and nuzzles underneath, stroking the satin fabric against her cheek. 'Mmm, lovely bed. Come and try it!'

Giggling, I jump into bed beside her. Doughnut stands there uncertainly, watching us. 'And you,' commands Rommy, holding the bedspread up and Doughnut's face clears and she hops into bed obediently, next to me. Rommy flings the bedspread over us all and we snuggle down together, laughing.

The next minute someone bangs on the door and we freeze. 'What's going on in there?' It's Zac, and I reckon he's up for joining in when he sees his girlfriend in bed with us, but we all holler at him to go away, Rommy included. This is strictly girl time. After he's taken himself off, we continue lying there for ages, fully clothed, with the bedspread over our heads, Rommy and me gossiping about Sophie and Hannah and what they were like chasing after those footie boys, and Doughnut taking it all in. After a while she starts to relax as she realizes that Rommy is not looking to jump down her throat after all (poor Rommy, as if she would!) and when we start discussing whether Mike and Donna are keen on each other she joins in. And, you know something? It's really nice and snug and cosy, the three of us, all yammering away, like we're all alone inside a tent in the middle of nowhere on a squally night.

We'd have been there till morning, I think, except Dad hammers on the door. 'Keep the noise down in there, you lot,' he says, 'I'm going to bed,' and we stop talking immediately, throw the bedspread back and pretend to be asleep. The door opens. I peek between my lids and see Dad taking us in, three sleeping bodies chastely in a line, like see no evil, hear no evil, speak no evil, only our heads visible, with the bedspread now primly tucked beneath our chins.

'Gosh,' I say, stretching and yawning flamboyantly. 'Hello, Dad. We must have fallen asleep. What time is it?'

'Late,' he says, but he sounds more amused than cross.

'I'd better wake Rommy up so we can get into my bed,' I hint loudly. 'Rommy?'

'Mmmm,' she says, wriggling comfortably and rubbing

her eyes, like she's going for an Oscar in pretend sleeping, 'I like it here, it's nice and comfy.'

'Might as well stay put then,' says Dad. 'Shame to disturb Sleeping Beauty there.' He gestures towards Doughnut who's doing a superb impression of a somnolent pig, complete with open jaw and soft, snuffly grunts. Rommy chuckles.

'Thanks, Mr Jamieson,' she says, sounding incredibly perky and awake all of a sudden. I dig her in the ribs and she remembers and yawns ostentatiously. 'Ooh,' she says, 'I'm tired.'

'Back to sleep then,' says Dad. 'Night, girls.'

'Night,' we all chorus, including Doughnut whose unfailing good manners make her forget she's supposed to be comatose. We bury our faces in the pillows to stop ourselves from giggling, but when Dad says, 'By the way, I'd get undressed if I were you, you'd be far more comfortable. At least, take your shoes off,' we give up all pretence and burst out laughing.

When Dad's gone we do as we're told. Sort of. We get undressed and into bed but then we lie awake for ages talking in muted voices. Lots of it is goss: who's said what about who (I know it should be whom!); who's in love with who (Rommy is with Zac, well I never!); who's fallen out with who. It's like by chatting about other people, we're finding out more about each other. But then we start getting into more serious stuff and Doughnut speaks about her mum and dad breaking up and what it felt like having to move house and start again in a new school and I feel uncomfortable because I know how hard I must have made it for her, even though she doesn't say so, and I change the subject quickly. After a while Rommy suddenly splutters out of the blue, 'Sleeping Beauty!' and Doughnut pretends to snore then does her funny bubbly laugh that sounds like a volcanic spring erupting and we're off again, and honestly, I swear we can't have gone to sleep much before dawn, but it doesn't matter, does it, because tomorrow's Sunday and there's no school and no gym either.

And here's the funny thing. Even though I've spent what little remained of the night squashed up between Rommy (who really does snore) and Doughnut (who flings her arms around), on Sunday morning I wake up and peer at them both, one on either side of me, still fast asleep, and I feel as refreshed as if I've slept for a week. I lie there quietly for a while, gazing around Amber's room, unfamiliar now, the floor buried under piles of discarded clothes and shoes, and bags with their contents spilling out all over the carpet, the dressing table awash with hairbrushes, combs, mounds of jewellery, mobile phones, used tissues with yesterday's make-up on them, pots of cream with open lids, and I listen to the steady breathing either side of me and I feel quiet, rested. Amid the chaos of this normally pristine room I feel . . . at peace.

'It's a mess, isn't it?' Doughnut is awake beside me finally.

'Yes, it is a bit.'

'What will Amber say?'

'Nothing.'

She doesn't believe me. 'I'll help you clean it up,' she says earnestly.

I turn my head and study her face on the pillow beside me. She's watching me, her brown eyes full of concern, the corner of her bottom lip caught between her even white teeth. I think about how mean I've been to her over the past weeks; I remember how she stuck up for me against the infamous Mr Minty; I think of the laugh we had last night then recall her disclosures about her parents splitting up and how she thought it was because of her, and I smile ruefully and stretch out my fist, pretending to punch her on the chin.

'Worry-guts. Amber won't give a stuff.'

'Why not?'

I sigh heavily. 'Because.'

'Because what?'

Just tell her. Say it out loud. Admit it at last. To her.

To yourself.

'Amber's dead.'

Doughnut's face is a picture. Her eyes are round with horror, her jaw has dropped and she's gone a livid shade of puce. I get this overwhelming urge to giggle, I can't help it, she looks so funny, like a character in a comic; all she needs is SHOCK! HORROR! coming out of her head in a big zigzag bubble. And to make it even more bizarre, on the other side of me, Rommy starts snoring again. (I'm going to tell Zac his girlfriend does a mean piggy impression.) A snigger escapes.

Doughnut goes mental. Her face contorts into a mask of fury and she sits bolt upright in bed and yells at me. Doughnut yell! It's me who's in shock now.

'THAT IS NOT FUNNY, EVA! I really believed you! How can you make a joke about something like that? You are seriously weird!'

'What's going on?' Rommy shoots up, scared witless, dragged from her dreams mid-snore. It occurs to me that if she was in the same comic strip her hair would be standing on end, but this time it's not quite as funny. 'What's all the shouting about?'

'Eva said her sister's dead!' spits out Doughnut, full of contempt. 'Freak!'

Wow, Doughnut, calm down! says my inner voice. I'm impressed, she's scary! She's obviously one of those people who's normally placid as anything but when they do lose it, watch out! Ben's a bit like that.

Poor Rommy. She's so distressed.

'Stop it, Doughnut!'

'Why should I?' She scowls at me as if she'd like to see *me* dead.

'Think about Eva!'

'I *am* thinking about Eva!' she says and her face screws up with anger. 'I'm thinking what a dreadful thing it is to say your own sister is dead!'

'So? Show a bit of sympathy! It's not her fault.'

Actually, it is, my inner voice pipes up again, but no one's listening, thank goodness. On one side of me Rommy is glaring at Doughnut and on the other side Doughnut's expression is undergoing transmutation from righteous moral outrage, through confusion, to dawning perception and, finally, dreadful comprehension. She looks from me to Rommy and back to me again, her mouth open.

'You mean . . . it's true?'

I nod.

'She's really . . .?' She swallows, unable to go on.

'Dead? Yes she is! You don't lie about something like that!' Rommy's normally good-natured face is ugly with disgust.

'I thought you were joking! Oh, Eva! I'm so sorry!'

'Like she'd joke about her own sister dying! Idiot! She doesn't even talk about it!' Rommy is beside herself. She gets out of bed and starts plucking clothes haphazardly off the floor, then she suddenly rolls them all up into a tight furious ball, bursts into tears and hurls them at Doughnut. They fall apart before they even reach her, but Doughnut lets out an agonized howl and clutches her face in her hands, as if she's been hit by a brick.

'What's going on in there?' yells Dad.

'We're just mucking about!' I shout back, then hiss, 'Doughnut, Rommy, shut up!' But Doughnut continues wailing and Rommy continues sobbing and the next thing, Ben starts thumping on the floor of his bedroom, which happens to be our ceiling. Then Zac bangs on the door shouting frantically, 'Rommy? Are you OK? Eva, what are you up to?' Like, thanks, Zac, I'm the only sane one in here! Through all the banging and shouting, Doughnut carries on bawling her head off, so loudly even Rommy stops crying and looks concerned, and briefly I consider sticking a pillow over her face, but lucky for her she turns over before I can put this plan into operation and buries herself in the pillows and the howls are muffled, then they turn into great shuddering sobs and eventually they cease altogether, and Zac goes back to his bedroom and Ben goes back to sleep and Dad goes grumbling downstairs to the kitchen to make himself a cup of tea. And peace is finally restored.

'Eva?'

Poor Doughnut is not a pretty sight. Her eyes are red and swollen, her nose is snotty and her face is blotched and bloated with all the tears she's shed. She's a bulbous, blobby jellyfish, quivering with mortification. Rommy, on the other hand, kind, soft-hearted Rommy, is a vicious little shrew, mean and hostile, prepared to defend me to the end. And both of them are gazing at me, like I know what to do next.

Weird, isn't it? I suppose if I'd ever thought about it, THE DAY I CAME OUT, the day I actually admitted Amber was dead, the day I finally spoke about her to my friends, then I would have imagined it would be a really sorrowful occasion with lots of hugging and holding hands, my mates united in being there for me, maybe the shedding of a quiet tear or two, cue sad music.

Joke! Instead of which, it's been totally mental. One mate doesn't even believe me and the other one picks a fight with her, there's a screaming match between them followed by, not just a tear or two, a blooming deluge more like. And now *I'm* left to pick up the pieces.

I can't help it. I know I'm asking for trouble. I know this is how it all started in the first place, with me giggling when I shouldn't have, but it's all so crazy, I can't help but see the funny side of it, especially when Doughnut says again in her little strangled voice, 'Eva? I'm soooo sorry.' I just burst out laughing and when I see her and Rommy's shocked faces, it makes me laugh even more.

'Come here, you big . . . doughnut,' I say and hold out my arms. 'And you, you daft bat. Can't have my two best mates falling out, can I?' Rommy makes it to me the same time as Doughnut falls into my arms, nearly knocking me flat in the process (sorry, I'm not being mean, I just can't help noticing these things), and we have a massive big hug, the three of us, which sounds nice but is actually a bit minging because both of them start blubbing again down my neck. Then Zac decides to investigate what's going on again, only this time he doesn't bother to knock, he just comes barging straight in and we all yell at him to get out again, including Rommy, who's more into bonding with her girlfriends at this precise moment. And when he sees us all laughing and crying together, he changes his mind anyway and exits as quickly as he came in.

Who says threesomes don't work?

When we've all stopped emoting and are on the bed again, me now wearing Amber's favourite hoodie over my jim-jams, I offer to have a go at Doughnut's hair with my straighteners while she flicks through a magazine. She could really do with it being cut into a new style. (One step at a time, Eva!) Rommy, wearing one of my sister's T-shirts, is sitting cross-legged, shaking up a bottle of nail varnish which has been solidifying on the dressing table for the past four years. Suddenly she stops in mid-shake and looks around the room, which, I have to admit, now, with the wardrobe doors wide open and clothes strewn around, looks less like Amber's bedroom, or at least, Amber's bedroom as Mum has kept it for the last four years, and more like a changing room at Topshop on Saturday afternoon.

Which, come to think of it, is what it always used to look like.

'What do you think Amber would have made of all this?' she asks.

'All what?'

'This.' She indicates the messy bed, the satin spread now creased and stained with something that looks suspiciously like nail varnish, the scattered clothes, the make-up, the magazines, the jewellery, the soggy tissues left over from the crying fest, the whole chaotic lot. 'And the shouting and crying and making up and all that stuff. All of it. Us.'

I stop and think for a minute, remembering Amber. Because she's gone now, she's not here any more, trapped in this mausoleum of a room. We've opened the door and let her out.

What *was* she like? I have to consciously think now.

Amber was gorgeous and she knew it. She'd sing and dance along to videos of her favourite bands, clutching a hairbrush as a microphone, and she had a tarty black lace bra that Mum knew nothing about. She had long tanned legs and she wore short skirts in summer and bright woolly tights in winter to show them off. She loved messing about with her hair, trying funky new styles, and she'd do mine too, for hours on end. Sometimes she'd put make-up on me and let me wear her jewellery; other times she'd yell at me to go away and stop touching her things. She was bossy and liked her own way and she always wanted the last word in an argument, but so did I so our arguments went on for ever. She was so impatient, she couldn't wait, everything had to be like, now! She wasn't tidy at all, she was messy, and she was kind and spiteful and loving and annoying and crazy and funny and larger than life and mad, mad, mad about gym and she was my sister, and I miss her dreadfully.

The tears roll down my cheeks.

'She'd have bloody loved it.'

Mum came home the day before the 4-Piece. By that time I'd moved into Amber's room. I'd cleared it with her first on the phone. Actually, I think Dad must have broached the subject to her already because she surprised me. She said, 'I think that's a very good idea.'

Rommy and Doughnut helped me move. We stripped the pink throw, the purple bedspread, the fluffy cushions and the soft toys off Amber's bed, we took the medals, the posters and the quilt with the badges off the wall, we pulled the neatly arranged CDs, tapes, videos and books off the shelves and dumped everything in a heap on my bed. Then we emptied the drawers and the wardrobe, bundling all Amber's clothes and shoes into big black bin-liners for recycling.

'Don't you want to keep any of these?' asked Rommy, trying a sparkly top up against herself.

'No thanks, there's only one thing I wanted and I've

already taken it. Help yourself. You too, Doughnut.'

Doughnut snorted. 'Like they'd fit me!'

Rommy admired herself in the full-length mirror, turning from side to side, considering, then suddenly she folded up the top and stuffed it decisively in the bin-liner.

'Nah, let it go to the charity shop, it's out of date anyway.'

'Sooo last season, darling,' I drawled.

'Or the one before.'

'Or the one before that!'

I giggled, then shook my head, and gazed in perplexity at the others. 'I can't believe Amber would ever be out of date. She was so funky.'

They stared back at me in solemn sympathy. 'I wish I'd met her,' said Rommy softly. 'Was she like you?'

I shrugged my shoulders. 'In some ways,' I said. 'Gym and that, obviously. And she was bolshie, like me. You know, she liked her own way.'

You know something? I'd never been asked that before, strangely enough. I'd only ever thought of it from the other angle, could I be like Amber? Could *I* be as good as her? Only it wasn't really so strange was it, because I'd never talked about my sister much to anyone, either inside the family or out. I'd talk *to* Amber, but not about her, because that way she wasn't really dead at all.

Mum knew, I'm sure she did. I think she probably did the same herself. Between us, we'd kept poor Amber stuck in this house for the past four years, a ghost that haunted both our lives.

I considered Rommy's question again. Was my sister like me or not?

'No she wasn't,' I said in surprise. 'She was Amber.'

'Your mum might not like it, you know, giving away your sister's stuff,' said Doughnut gently.

'We'll leave it all in my old room till she comes home.' I crammed the last of the clothes into the bag and twisted the top into a knot. 'Then she can do what she wants with it. Come on, give us a hand getting my gear in.'

Between the three of us, it didn't take long. Actually, it was Doughnut who did most of it: she sprang to life like a flipping gang-master, directing operations. Before I knew it, I was moved lock, stock and barrel into my brand-new room with all my own things tidied away neatly, pictures positioned with mathematical precision on the wall, CDs and books standing to attention on the shelves, and my THIS SEASON clothes either hanging obediently in the wardrobe or folded sternly into drawers by Doughnut (they wouldn't stay like that for long!), with just my particular all-time favourites like my old grey hoodie and the Joseph and the Amazing Technicolor Dreamcoat dressing gown I had for

Christmas when I was ten, allowed by Patty (just call me Trinny and Susannah) Williams to hang on the back of the door as long as they behaved themselves. She even told me to get rid of some of *my* stuff to the charity shop, blooming cheek!

The funny thing was, I did as I was told.

And then the BEST THING HAPPENED! Rommy and I were making the bed up with my own sheets and duvet leaving Doughnut to poke about in the bottom of Amber's (I mean, my new) wardrobe, lining up my shoes in neat pairs (What *is* her problem? Obsessive or what?), when suddenly she said, 'What on earth is this?' and held something aloft. It was a grotty old piece of cloth, scruffy, grey and dingy-looking, and Rommy said automatically, 'Bin it,' but I yelled, 'NO!'

I recognized it immediately, you see, and my heart missed a beat. I grabbed it off her before it could be consigned to the bin-bag with the rest of the rubbish and clutched it to my nose with both hands, inhaling deeply. OK, it smelt a bit rank if I was honest, and when I examined it closely there were patches of black mould that had eaten away holes in the wool in places, but the satin edge was still intact and as I stroked its shiny smoothness I knew there was no way I was ever going to let it go again.

'What is it?' asked Rommy, puzzled.

'It's my Piece of Cold,' I said, dizzy with happiness.

'Your what?'

'My Piece of Cold.' *(A piece of cold: an article that calms, comforts and consoles; a cloth that is reassuring and soothing; a woollen blanket with a satin edge that brings Eva peace.)*

Doughnut smiled at me. 'It's your old comfort blanket, isn't it? I had one of those.'

'Aahh.' Rommy's brow cleared. 'I get it. I wonder what it was doing in Amber's wardrobe?'

'It was in the corner, under the lining,' explained Doughnut, looking to see if there was anything else lurking in the recesses of the wardrobe.

Amber! I knew it! So that's where you hid it. I buried my face in its softness so my mates couldn't see me grinning and whispered, 'Minger!'

Then I listened, as hard as I could, straining with the effort, but there was no reply. Not a 'Creep!' Not a 'Psycho!' Nothing.

'What did you say?' asked Doughnut, backing her way out of the wardrobe and sitting up on her heels. 'There we are. All finished. What do you think?'

'How do you like your new bedroom?' Rommy's face was apprehensive.

My eyes swept the room and returned to her and Doughnut, both of them looking anxious. I smiled.

'It's ace. Thank you, for all you've done. Both of you.'

I stroked my Piece of Cold against my cheek and gave a huge sigh of contentment. 'It feels like mine now.'

When I come home from school the night before the competition, Mum's already there. She opens the front door to me as I'm inserting the key into the lock and I literally fall into her arms. I've forgotten what it feels like to be hugged by her, what she smells like, and we stand together for ages, rocking gently, drinking each other in. At last, she holds me at arms' length.

'Oh my goodness, Eva!' she says. 'You've lost so much weight!'

'No I haven't!' I say automatically, then add, 'Well, just a bit.' She hugs me again and this time I feel her hands on my back, first on my shoulder blades, then, not very subtly, moving down to my ribcage and all of a sudden I'm aware of how much my bones jut out and I pull away. 'I've been busy training for the competition,' I say in justification, 'and I've been running a lot, that's all. I'm fine, Mum, honest.'

She studies me carefully, but says nothing. Soon the boys come in and there are more hugs, then Dad appears from the kitchen where he's cooking supper, with a celebratory bottle of bubbly and some glasses. He shakes the bottle and points it at us, pushing the cork with his thumb, and it shoots across the lounge and ricochets off the wall to hit me on the nose and everyone shrieks with laughter. Ben just about manages to get a glass underneath before it spills all over the carpet, and then we all toast Mum and swig our champagne, except for me who takes a sip and says, 'Uggh!' because it's too sweet and fizzy, and everyone laughs again.

'Anyway,' I say defensively, 'I don't want to do the 4-Piece with a hangover, do I?'

'We should have kept the champagne for tomorrow,' says Mum, her eyes sparkling. 'When Eva gets the gold.'

'We'll have another bottle then,' says Ben. 'Any left, Dad?' He holds out his glass for more but Mum whisks it away.

'Slow down! You're drinking too much, my boy!'

She's laughing but Ben knows she means it. Mum's back in charge again. I'm glad.

'*If* Eva gets the gold,' I correct her.

Mum nods and her eyes become serious. 'I can't wait to see your floor routine. Are you pleased with it?'

'So-so.'

'Rommy says it's really good,' says Zac.

'It's OK.'

I wish they'd change the subject.

'Champagne, my supper cooked . . . you know, I think I'll have to go away more often,' says Mum as if she's read my mind, and the attention moves back to her. At suppertime we sit down to steak and chips (Dad's repertoire is quite restricted, as I've discovered) and I can feel her watching me, so I make a colossal effort to force chunks of dead cow down my throat, by cutting it up really small, but it still makes me heave and I push most of it under the chips and nibble at the salad instead. She takes the plates away and doesn't say a thing, but I know she's noticed.

After supper she says, 'Ben? Haven't you got some revision to do?' Ben looks a bit surprised as if he's forgotten what the word means, but disappears to his room without a murmur. The rest of us watch telly for a bit, Mum and I cuddled up on the sofa together, her arms around me, till I decide it's time to go up.

'Big day tomorrow,' she says. 'We're looking forward to it, aren't we Zac?'

'Are you coming?' I stare at him in surprise.

' 'Course,' says Zac. 'It's the big one, isn't it? Can't miss you strutting your stuff.'

'Yeah, right!' I snort. 'Can't miss the lovely Rommy more like.'

'Her too. You're coming as well, aren't you, Dad? And Ben,' he adds with a grin.

'Ben's coming? To see me?'

He chuckles. 'To eye up the talent, I reckon. Ever since

he met your friend Doughnut, he's suddenly become interested in gym.'

'Is that his game? Eva's friends are far too young for Ben!' says Mum indignantly.

'I'm joking! He's coming to watch Eva!' says Zac, but he winks at me behind Mum's back.

'Well, it's nice to see you all taking an interest at last,' says Mum. 'Now you make sure you get a good night's sleep, Eva. I'll be up in a minute to tuck you in.'

'Ah, diddums,' says Zac and I flick his ear hard as I go past. 'Ouch!'

'You're only jealous.'

Upstairs I snuggle down into bed with my Piece of Cold. It hasn't lost its power at all, in fact I reckon it must have built up even more over the years it spent hidden away at the bottom of Amber's wardrobe, because I'm practically asleep by the time Mum comes up. It's not till I feel her sit on my bed and smooth my hair back that I'm even aware she's there.

'Look at you,' she says, tugging gently at the corner of the satin strip nestled beneath my cheek. 'Where did that old thing come from?'

'Amber's wardrobe,' I say drowsily. 'She'd hidden it in there.'

'Little madam,' she chuckles. 'I remember now. She must have had it all the time! Looks as if it could do with a good wash.'

I turn over to face her. She's gazing down at me, a strange expression in her eyes.

'She was no angel, Eva. She wasn't perfect, you know,' she says softly. 'And you don't have to be either.'

'I'm not.' My chest is painful, like there's a huge weight inside, trying to force its way out, and suddenly it's hard to breathe, let alone talk.

Mum frowns and strokes my cheek with the back of her hand. 'What's the matter, Eva? What is it?'

'Nothing.'

'Don't you feel well?'

'I'm fine.'

'Are you worried about tomorrow?'

'No.'

'It's OK, you can tell me what's troubling you.'

The dam bursts.

'It was me,' I moan. 'It was all my fault.'

'What was?'

'Nothing. Go away.' I turn away and bury my face in the pillow, sobbing, but she pulls me back.

'Eva! Tell me what's wrong.'

'That day,' I sob, '. . . when Amber died . . .'

'Yes?'

'It was me. I did it. I killed her.'

She gasps, her eyes filling with horror.

She hates me. I knew she would.

'Eva!'

'I'm sorry, Mum! I'm really sorry!' The tears roll down my cheeks and my chest hurts like it's been ripped open. I cry like I've never cried before in my whole life.

She puts her arms around me and she cries too.

Afterwards we talk, for ages, late into the night, long after everyone else has gone to bed. Well, actually, that's not quite true. We don't talk all the time, there are gaps when we just lie there together on the bed, my back resting securely against Mum, my bottom sitting comfortably on her knees, like she's a high chair and her arms wrapped around me are the reins, keeping me safely strapped in.

We do talk though, about important stuff that we've both kept bottled up for a long time. Then our conversation is like Dad's champagne, the cork pops and out it all pours in a fizzling, foaming torrent. It turns out while that I've spent years blaming myself for Amber's death, Mum has been blaming herself too.

'It was me that was being naughty in the back of the car,' I explain.

'You were always naughty. All of you were. You were

kids. Being naughty doesn't mean you're responsible for Amber dying.'

'I opened my lunchbox and sprayed guacamole all over the place.'

'Oh, Eva.' Mum hugged me tight. 'Guacamole didn't kill her. A car crash did. And I was driving.' I can feel her tears again, cold on the back of my neck, like a baptism, washing away my guilt, absolving me from my sin.

'It wasn't your fault either, Mum.'

'No,' she sighs deeply. 'I know that now, but it's taken Dr Beerbaum to help me come to terms with it.'

We lapse back into silence again. Against the base of my spine I can feel her stomach rising and falling imperceptibly and her breath wafts against my hair, stirring it gently. I feel utterly at peace.

'Do you talk to her, Eva?'

'I used to, all the time.'

'I did too.'

'She's gone now.'

'I know, I can tell. We've let her go.'

There's a pause, then Mum says, 'Better let you get to sleep, young lady. Competition tomorrow. Are you nervous?'

'No.' It's true, I'm not. 'But I don't know how I'm going to do.'

'Just try your best.' She leans over and gives me kiss. 'Can't do better than that.'

'Mum?'

'Yes?'

'I don't think I'll ever be as good as Amber.'

She pauses. 'You're Eva, not Amber. It's not a competition.'

'Yes it is!'

We giggle. Then she says, 'Love you, Eva. Sleep well.'

I sleep like a baby.

When I came out of hospital after the accident I remember running down the garden to go on the swing, glad to be home and free again. Years ago, Dad had hung a rope over the branch of the big sycamore and attached an old tyre to it. We spent more time squabbling over that swing than actually playing on it, Amber and me, all the usual stuff like 'My go!' 'No, it's mine!' 'You've been on it for ages!' I climbed on to it and pushed off hard with my legs, trying to get a momentum going, but it was no good, I didn't have the strength to do it. I had that swing all to myself and it wasn't going anywhere. I cried and Dad rushed out and gave me a push. He thought I was missing Amber, and I was, but that's not the reason I was crying; she wouldn't have pushed me anyway, she'd have told me to get off and let her have a go instead. No, it was because I felt so tired, so tired and weak I couldn't even bend backwards and drive myself up into the sky, something I'd been able to do for years. I didn't feel like me at all, I felt like a very old person, feeble and exhausted.

That's what I feel like this morning when I wake up. I'm aching with weariness.

'Breakfast?' asks Mum when I come downstairs, then she takes one look at me and adds, 'Or just a cup of tea?'

'You look terrible,' says Zac, who's busy shovelling cereal down his throat for England. 'Have you got a hangover?'

'Very funny,' I groan. 'I'm just knackered. I'll be fine when I come round.'

'Try and eat something,' says Mum, placing the steaming tea in front of me. 'Piece of toast?'

I shake my head but she puts it in front of me anyway and stands guard while I nibble at it with little enthusiasm. My phone bleeps. It's Rommy wishing me good luck. I text her back, 'Go, Jimmies!' and send it to Doughnut as well and, then, as an afterthought, Sophie and Hannah. Soon my phone is bleeping away manically and the tea and toast does the trick and I start to perk up and look forward to the day.

The 4-Piece is being held in the next town, ten miles away. When Mum's braided my hair (Ouch! Too tight, Mum!), Dad's back from his run and Ben has been dug out of his pit, we set off, me squashed in the back between Ben and Zac, not a pleasant experience. I don't know if it's the fetid odour of unwashed teen boy emanating from Ben on one side of me (OK, I'm exaggerating!) or the overpowering pungency of Zac's enthusiastic shower-gelled, shampooed, deodorized, must-impress-my-girlfriend, early morning ablutions on the other (I'm definitely *not* exaggerating!), plus the fact that Mum's braids are so tight my scalp feels it's been stretched on a rack, but by the time we get there, I've got a blinding headache. At least I'm past caring whether everyone will think I'm a loser, turning up with my whole family in tow.

Inside, the place is teeming. Six clubs are taking part and I don't know what I'm worrying about, it looks like everyone's brought their own personal fan club with them. Dad and the boys grab some seats and Mum and I head for the familiar blue and yellow tracksuits milling round on the floor amongst a sea of colours, picking our way over bodies, sleeping bags, discarded tracksuits, bottles of water and bags of provisions till we reach their sides.

'Hi, Mrs Jamieson!' says Rommy. There's no sign of the rest of the Jimmies, but everyone else seems to be here.

'Lorna!' shrieks Donna and hugs Mum. 'How're you doing?'

'Great,' smiles Mum. 'Going to be a good day?'

'Hope so. The under 13s are shaping up nicely; the

under 12s, hmm, bit iffy. We've got a cracking team in the under 15s though. Eva never lets us down . . . and the new girl, Doughnut, she's come on a treat.'

'Doughnut . . .' Mum laughs and shakes her head.

'There's a story to that . . .'

'Hello, gorgeous.' Mike kisses Mum on the cheek. 'Going to do a warm-up for us?'

Everyone's pleased to see Mum, who's being treated like a minor celeb, and nobody's noticing me so I wander back to where Dad and the boys are sitting. So much for my fan club. They've picked a good seat but they're paying zilch attention to what's going on in the gym: Rommy's beaten me to it and has entwined herself around Zac like a piece of bindweed, Ben's gone back to sleep and Dad's reading the paper and making a start on the pile of cheese and pickle sarnies Mum's brought with her to sustain my energy. Go, Dad, I can't eat a thing anyway. I glance towards the entrance. No sign of Sophie and Hannah yet, they're cutting it fine, but Doughnut and her mum have just come in and are standing there uncertainly. I wave to them and they make their way towards us. Ben opens his eyes, spots Doughnut and sits up quickly, budging up for her mum to sit down. He's *so* obvious.

I take a sip of water and pass the bottle to Doughnut. 'Ben fancies you,' I whisper.

She splutters mid-swig. 'Get lost!'

'He does!'

She looks pink and pleased. Am I missing something here? What *is* the attraction my brothers hold for my mates? Don't they realize the stuff teenage boys strut to the world is a mask and in the privacy of their own home they're feral? Their lives are ruled by a silly ball being chased around a field, their feet stink, and gorging, belching and farting appear to be high on the list of their preferred activities.

Apparently not.

I sigh. I don't think I'll ever fancy anyone, I know too much about men. It's a pain having brothers, they're arresting my sexual development.

'Are you serious, Eva? Does he really like me?'

'Yes! How many times? Why don't you believe me?'

'Why don't I believe you? Mmm . . .' She strikes a pose. 'I wonder why? Because banana cake and carrot cake and baked potatoes drowning in half a kilogram of cheese are really slimming, aren't they? Oh yes, and who was it who gave me the name Doughnut? My mum thinks it was Rommy. Then there's the small matter of bleep tests . . .'

It's my turn to go red. 'I'm sorry,' I whisper. 'D'you hate me?'

'Just a bit,' she says and my heart plummets but then

she grins and says, 'Not any more,' and enfolds me to her, and we squeeze each other so tight I can't breathe and now I can't stop grinning either. At last she straightens up.

'Look, your mum's calling us. It's time to warm up. Zac! Put Rommy down, she's needed.'

'Where's Hannah and Sophie?'

'They're coming. Look, over there.'

I spot the pair of them battling their way towards us through the crowd. Quickly I turn to Doughnut. 'I mean it, you know. He does like you, it's obvious. He's come to watch you, not me.'

'Heck.' She giggles nervously. 'I hope I don't mess up then!'

Down on the floor the coaches from the various clubs are talking through the competition with their respective teams. Hannah and Sophie sidle into place beside us and Mike gives them a baleful look, but continues with his pep talk. Then we go straight into warm-up with Donna putting us through our paces while Mum and Mike take the younger ones. I run through my floor exercise, still feeling a bit below par, though my headache's starting to fade. I'll be all right once I get going.

Soon it's time for the competition to begin. We line up in order of height, ready to parade on, me last but one, with Doughnut behind me, and the music starts. I love this bit, your head goes up, your chin juts out and you parade around the floor one behind the other, back straight, arms swinging, toes and fingers pointed, stepping out to the beat of the music and anything is possible. Then, when your team is introduced, you step forward together and salute to the judges and cheers go up from your section of the audience and you can't wait to start.

We've got to contain our patience though, the under 12s are on first. Our team's OK, but they're not as keen as we were at that age (how middle-aged does that sound?) and some of the performances are a bit ragged. Mike looks glum. The under 13s are much better. A couple of the girls have really come on, they must be in line for medals, and he starts to look more cheerful. In the past I've always sat with the Jimmies watching other girls compete, usually, if I'm honest, making snide remarks about their performance. But today is different, I sit by Mum and we follow the competition together, commenting on each individual girl's performance objectively, like equals. It's good.

'You're very knowledgeable,' whispers Doughnut's mum to me and I smile modestly and say, 'I've been doing it for years!' but inside I'm chuffed. It's flattering to be recognized as an expert, especially when she leans over and says to Mum, 'Eva's been so helpful to Patty, you know, training her up for this competition.' Mum smiles at me proudly and I feel my face glowing with pleasure. This is a new one for me, getting credit for helping someone. It's a nice feeling.

Soon it's lunchtime and Mum tries to encourage me to eat a sandwich but I can't, though I do manage a drink of water. 'Patty doesn't want much either,' says Doughnut's mum consolingly. 'I expect it's nerves.' Doughnut smiles sympathetically and helps herself to another of my cheese and pickle sarnies.

We divide up into four groups. I'm on the vault first, and though this is the one I've been practising for ages, the Yurchenko, Mike's decided I should go for a half-on, full twist-off handspring for my first vault, just to make sure I've got points on the scoreboard. I run up fast, place my arms against the vault, push up with my legs and rotate my heels over my head, twisting my body as I fly over the apparatus to land squarely on both feet. Textbook stuff. A cheer goes up from our benches.

When I walk back for my second vault, I know what I have to do. I've been doing it in my sleep, not always successfully though. The gym falls silent, word's got round I'm attempting the Yurchenko. I take a deep breath, go up on my toes and sprint towards the horse. Bit too fast, Eva. My feet pound on to the springboard and I push myself up into a backward handspring, then use my hands to spin into first one, then another half somersault before making a less controlled landing than I'd planned, staggering slightly. Weeks of practice and it's over in seconds. I look up. Mike's on his feet, clapping loudly and grinning from ear to ear, and the gym erupts into a tumult of applause. It's OK. I smile and give a pert salute to the judges.

I get a chance to watch Rommy before we move on to the asymmetric bars. The vault is not her favourite but she manages two respectable half and halves and wins thunderous applause from Zac. The bars are my speciality, I've got the strength and flexibility to keep the routine flowing. So far in this competition nobody seems anywhere near my standard. When it's my turn, I wait patiently for the signal from the judges, giving Mum a quick glance. She's sitting upright and her eyes are glued to me.

At last I'm allowed to start and I leap into action, grabbing the high bar and sweeping myself up. I build up momentum and fly between the bars, high on adrenalin, circling, swinging, releasing and catching, like a trapeze artist. But then, surprisingly, in mid-move, I find a handstand an effort, and I'm forced to do an extra swing which I know will cost me points and I realize, surprisingly, I'm tiring. It's not long now, Eva, keep going, I tell myself and I grit my teeth and force my body to obey, and now it hurts, my arms, my neck, my back, my legs, everywhere. The last five seconds are pure agony, but at last I let go of the bar and sail forward to land on my feet and I straighten up and salute triumphantly and it's over. The crowd cheer. I've done it.

But I know I couldn't have done it for a second more.

'Well done,' says Mike, patting me on the shoulder. 'You OK?'

I nod, trying to catch my breath.

'Tired?'

'A bit.'

'Come and watch this. Doughnut's about to do her floor routine.'

We walk over to the area where Doughnut is poised, deep in concentration, ready to begin. The familiar music starts up and she's off, leaping into action. The crowd wakes up and starts clapping in time to the music as she bounces diagonally across the floor, making the relatively simple tumble sequences Mike has put together for her look totally amazing. I don't know how she does it, I really don't. Other people in the competition have done far more complicated moves, but she's just bursting with energy and so fluid, so controlled, so dynamic, so *beautiful* to watch it's just magic, and the crowd thinks so too, because by the end, when she sinks to the floor with her chin on her hands and grins cheekily at everyone, they're on their feet and cheering so loud the noise echoes round the building.

'Was it OK?' asks Doughnut anxiously as she comes off the floor. She glances up at the crowd and spots Ben standing up clapping with his hands above his head and her face breaks into a smile.

'I think you've just broken the sound barrier,' beams Mike and gives her a hug.

My next apparatus is the balance beam. Rommy and I both like this; me because I'm good at balancing, Rommy because she can show off her years of dance training, so today I feel confident as I start my piece with a jump to handstand and then lower myself to straddle. But then, when I go into my backward walkover, something I've done countless times before, I suddenly feel strange, kind of light-headed, and I wobble a bit as I come out of it. A gasp goes up from the spectators, but I manage to stay on. I pause for a bit till my head clears then I move into my arabesque and hold it for two seconds and that's fine, but as soon as I put my head down to do a forward roll along the beam I can feel myself getting dizzy again. I manage somehow, through sheer determination, to complete my routine without falling off but I know I've had some fairly major wobbles along the way which will have cost me valuable points.

'Are you OK?' asks Rommy as I sit back down beside her on the mat. I shake my head.

'I don't know. I feel weird.' I put my head between my knees. Mike comes over and squats down beside me.

'Feeling giddy?' he asks.

I nod.

'Did you have breakfast this morning?'

I think back. 'A piece of toast.'

'What do you expect?' he asks grimly.

Over on the asymmetric bars, Sophie is struggling. At one point she falls off and lands in a heap on the mat. Mike thrusts a sandwich into my hand. 'Eat it!' he orders. 'You need the energy!' I lift the curling edge of the white bread to peer at the cooked ham inside it in disgust. It's got a rind of white fat all around it and is coated in yellow butter. I can't eat that. 'She looks as if she could do with a good night's sleep!' he mutters, scowling at Sophie. Hannah's next. She's marginally better, at least she doesn't fall off, but when she completes her routine there's only a smattering of applause.

'How are we doing?' I ask, but he shakes his head.

'I'm not checking the scores,' he says, then adds, 'The opposition's not up to much.' But he's looking more and more fed up by the minute until Rommy manages to pull off a clean, perky routine on the beam and bring a smile to his face at last.

It's our turn on the floor next. I get rid of the sandwich surreptitiously, hiding it under an abandoned pair of trackie pants, having taken a few tiny token bites. I'm sooo embarrassed when I notice Mike picking it up with a frown and depositing it in the bin.

I've been looking forward to this. Let's face it, the floor is what women's gymnastics is all about. When you think of the great names from the past, Olga Korbut and Nadia Comaneci, it's their floor routines you remember. And today I intend to pull off my own Perfect 10.

I get into position. My music is catchy, fast and aggressive, like me, and people start clapping to the beat before I even begin. Good sign, I can feel them lifting me as I spring into my first tumble. I know this routine by heart, every move, every dance step, I've done it so many times I could do it in my sleep, and I leap from one sequence to the next without a pause.

But, here's the thing, halfway through it and I'm tiring again, I don't know what's happening to me today, it's never happened before. For goodness' sake, Eva, pull yourself together, there's only a half a minute to go! But I'm feeling so weak, my arms ache and the muscles in my legs feel as if they've lost their tension and have turned to jelly. I force myself into my front somi and pull it off but it's flat and now it's all just too much effort. I can sense the clapping falling away and now I have to do my new move, my grand finale, my pièce de résistance, the handspring with full twist. I make an extra-special effort and leap as high as I can, pushing into the floor with my hands, but it's not enough, I can't get the twist in. I try to land squarely but I've overextended and I stagger and my stupid jelly legs won't support me. I fall over backwards and the crowd groans.

I've blown it.

I'm out of time now. The music stops and I get up and salute to the judges, old trouper that I am, and walk off the floor to a rousing round of applause. I don't bother going back to the mat. I'm finished anyway, I go straight back to Mum who puts her arm around me and squeezes me tight.

'Are you all right?' she whispers.

I nod. I am, strangely enough. I'm simply too tired to care. I watch the rest of the competition from the protective circle of Mum's arm, slumped against her, numb with exhaustion. The only time I stir is when Doughnut manages to get through her asymmetric bars routine without mishap and then I sit up and clap enthusiastically, knowing all too well the weeks of effort it's taken for her to get to grips with this discipline. Life is weird. Only a month or two ago, I'd have been praying she'd have fallen off them into a pit and disappeared for ever.

At the end Mike comes over.

'How are you feeling?' he asks.

Mum places her hand on my brow. 'She's wiped out,' she says worriedly. 'I wonder if she's got a dose of flu? Or glandular fever maybe? That drains your energy. I think I'd better take her to the doctor's.'

Mike nods. 'Good idea,' he says. 'Find out what's up, hey?' He makes a fist and taps me on the knee. 'You did good.'

'Thanks.' I know he's lying. 'Are we in the medals?'

'Bound to be,' he says cheerily.

I'm not convinced.

He's right though. The Jimmies sweep the board between them and win the overall team gold. Well, not Sophie, she doesn't do so well. In fact, it turns out she's the one whose scores don't count, as it happens. Too many late nights out with her footie boyfriend, I guess.

'I'm not bothered,' she pouts. 'Actually, I think I'm bit too mature for gym nowadays.'

Yeah, right.

The rest of us manage to come up trumps though. Hannah wins a bronze on the bars; Rommy gets the individual gold on the beam to her and Zac's noisy delight, and a silver on the vault; I get bronze on the beam (those flipping wobbles!), silver on the floor surprisingly (despite my flat front somi and catastrophic fall, I suppose I pick up marks for level of difficulty), silver on the bars (narrowly missing out to a girl from the host club, I lost 0.3 marks for that extra swing, boo hoo!) and gold on the vault (three cheers for the Yurchenko!). Better than I expected.

It's Doughnut who pulls off the surprise of the day though. She wins the bronze on the vault, with a half and half of all things.

And she gets the gold on the floor.

Rommy, Doughnut and I are in my bedroom. It's become a bit of a meeting place for the Jimmies nowadays, including Hannah and Sophie, now the footie lads have dumped them. Sophie tried to get Hannah to give up gym too but Hannah's all motivated again now she's beaten her in competition, so Sophie's drifted back and I've noticed she's putting a bit more effort in lately. She's like me, she doesn't like being second best.

It was hard, I admit it, when Doughnut beat me on the floor. Mike had a chat with me about it the other day.

'Gymnastics is all about perfection,' he said, warming to his favourite theme. 'It's better to do simple moves perfectly . . .'

'. . . than mess up on complicated moves,' I finish for him.

He grins. 'Have I said this before?'

'Just once or twice.'

'Don't take it too hard, Eva. Doughnut had a good tutor.'

'Big-head!'

'I mean you, idiot!' His face becomes serious. 'You ought to do a coaching course, you know. You'd be really good at it.'

'You reckon?'

He nods emphatically. 'Think about it.'

'Maybe.'

I have thought about it. I think he's right. I would be good at it. I love telling people what to do!

It's Saturday afternoon and Hannah and Sophie are out shopping for something to wear tonight. We're all going to the gym club presentation evening and there's a disco afterwards. Sophie's on a mission to replace her errant boyfriend and I think she's got her eyes on Jason again. Maybe she'll be in with a chance this time. I was wrong, he's definitely not gay.

He can't be or he wouldn't have asked me out after the 4-Piece.

I said no. I don't fancy him, I think he's slimy.

Still, it was nice to be asked.

I must let Sophie know sometime.

We're trying on clothes for tonight. I'm going to wear my old favourite, skinny jeans and my black strappy top. It looks OK again now I've put a bit of weight back on.

Mum ended up taking me to the doctor's after the

competition. I didn't have glandular fever as it turned out; I didn't even have flu. I was simply, slowly but surely, starving myself to death. Well, OK, it wasn't quite that serious but it could have been if I'd kept on the way I was going. I'd lost pounds and pounds and my blood sugar levels were all over the place. I never mentioned this before but my periods had stopped too. No wonder I was weak and dizzy and had no energy.

I realize now how potentially serious it was and I'm trying to eat more, though I get fed up with Mum watching me like a hawk all the time. There's no quick-fix solution, it's not that simple. I go for counselling now (like mother, like daughter) and it seems to be working, but there are no guarantees. But I'm starting to understand how I got into this situation. It's all to do with Amber and how I blamed myself for her dying and tried to compensate by being the daughter Mum had lost.

Crazy, hey? I guess that's what that dream was trying to tell me but I was too scared to listen. I never did work out if I was trying to catch up with Amber or if I was running away from her, but what the hell? I don't have it any more. I guess I've run full circle.

Rommy's trying on a pink vest top and a white mini skirt. 'How's this?'

'Fantastic. Zac will love you anyway, whatever you're wearing. You could go in a bin-bag for all he'd care.'

She piles her hair on top of her head and pouts at herself in the mirror. 'Down or up?'

'Down,' I say.

'Up,' says Doughnut simultaneously, her voice emerging from inside a dress that she's trying on. I giggle and help her to pull it down over her head and shoulders. She tugs it round, smoothing it over her hips and tummy, and examines herself critically in the mirror. 'What do you think?'

'It's fabulous.' I mean it. It's a dark-blue shiny material and it clings to her body.

'You look sensational,' says Rommy.

'Voluptuous,' I add.

'Does that mean fat?'

'No!' I'm telling the truth. 'It means sexy.'

'That's all right then.' Doughnut looks pink and pleased. 'I'm not exactly a perfect size 10 though, am I?'

'No,' I say honestly. 'But you're a perfect size 12.'

'Perfect size 14 or 16, more like,' grumbles Doughnut, but she doesn't look bothered. She stands sideways and stares at her reflection then pushes her breasts up. 'I need a new bra.'

'Well, I declare!' I say, adopting a pseudo Southern American drawl. 'I have the very thing!' I rummage around in the bottom of my underwear drawer and pull out a tarty-looking black lace bra and chuck it at her. 'Try that on for size!'

'I can't wear this!' squeals Doughnut, unzipping her dress and pulling it on nevertheless.

'Yes you can. It fits you perfectly!'

The door opens and Mum puts her head around. 'Cup of tea downstairs if you want it.' Her eyes fall on Doughnut. 'Oh my goodness!' she says. Her head disappears abruptly and the door closes. Doughnut's face is a picture.

'She thinks I'm a tart!' she wails. 'She'll tell my mum!'

Rommy and I explode laughing.

'I don't care,' says Doughnut, zipping her dress back up. 'It's fabulous. Look,' she runs her hands down her silhouette, 'it makes all the difference. Where did you get it from?'

'It was Amber's.'

'Did it fit her?'

'In her dreams!' I pause. 'It's the one thing I've kept of hers. Don't let Ben see you in it. You'll drive him wild!'

Rommy scrabbles about in the bottom of her bag. 'Don't know about a cup of tea, I'm starving. Yes!' She holds a bar of chocolate up triumphantly then chucks it to me. 'Eva, do the honours, there's a good girl.'

I snap it into three even pieces, one each for me and my best friends. Well, more or less even. I reserve the largest piece for me, of course. It's not easy to change the habits of a lifetime.

Anyway, I never said I was Little Miss Perfect.